THE SIEGE
And Other Award
Winning Stories

THE SIEGE

AND OTHER AWARD WINNING STORIES

ESTHER NEWTON

SilverWood

Published in 2014 by the author
using SilverWood Books Empowered Publishing®

SilverWood Books Ltd
30 Queen Charlotte Street, Bristol, BS1 4HJ
www.silverwoodbooks.co.uk

ISBN 978-1-78132-310-6 (paperback)
ISBN 978-1-78132-262-8 (ebook)

British Library Cataloguing in Publication Data
A CIP catalogue record for this book is available from
the British Library

Set in Sabon by SilverWood Books
Printed on responsibly sourced paper

*For Granny Mo, Pops, Mark and Charlotte... who
inspired me to never give up and to achieve my dreams.*

*A debt of gratitude to The Writers Bureau, where
my creative journey began and for giving me the
opportunity to help others realise their dreams.*

*Also a special mention to SilverWood Books for their
support, putting up with my endless questions
and for making my book a reality.*

Contents

The Siege

I didn't think sieges happened in libraries. Banks and building societies – yes. I could understand a jeweller's, too. But not a library. And it's all my fault.

We've been in this little room for ages now – him and me. The phone has rung twice, but he won't let me answer it. He just shakes his head and waves his gun around. I feel I should say something, but I don't know what to say.

I look at him – at his eyes flitting from side to side and lips, white where he keeps chomping on them. His brows dance up and down, seemingly unsure whether to rise into the shock of a surprise or to furrow into a frown. He sniffs, sucking in his nostrils and then they flare out like a dragon about to unleash a flurry of flames.

I swallow. This is the first time I've been afraid of him. Him. I don't even know his name. I didn't take the time to ask him or to even care. He was just there, every Monday morning, waiting outside for the doors to open.

I should have known that there was something different about him. I did, though only to a certain extent. He didn't ever borrow any books. Not that he was the only one. Lots of people like to come and browse or to look up references. But he didn't even do that.

"I see you've got yourself an admirer, Lesley," Shirley always teased.

I had laughed with her at first. Of course he wasn't. Then I would catch him staring at me.

"I'd watch him if I were you. He's a bit of a weirdo, that one," Shirley said, after finding him stroking a book I had just put back on a shelf.

"He's not doing any harm," I said back.

And he wasn't. Not really. Deep down I was a little flattered, especially when he bought me some flowers. Well, there were more weeds than flowers, but no one had ever bought me flowers before. It seemed so thoughtful. I've always loved flowers. My house is full of them – all bought by myself from the local garden centre. So I went home that night and put my admirer's into water, alongside the carnations and chrysanthemums.

I suppose I felt sorry for him. I could see him at school – the little one at the back with hand-me-down clothes that didn't fit, with hair hanging down over his eyes as he stared out the window, wondering if his mum and dad would ever stop rowing. I could see him so clearly, almost as clearly as me. I was the little one at the back, too, with my three sisters' hand-me-down clothes, which were always far too big, with my fringe falling in my face and my eyes far away, thinking about Mum throwing last night's supper at Dad. I wasn't pretty, clever, sporty or fun to be with. I was the loner, too.

I could have turned out like him and taken childhood trauma into my adult years. I didn't. Perhaps it was my new stepdad that made all the difference, giving me extra tuition or my eldest sister trying out her newly acquired beautician skills on me. Maybe it was going off to university or I like to think that a lot of it was down to me.

Though, when I saw him, I saw some of that little girl, too. I'd had chances and opportunities. He obviously hadn't. But I didn't think it would lead to this. To his marching into the library this morning and taking me by the hand. His touch was unexpected – soft, gentle and there was a kindness in his eyes as they looked into mine. Then, in one motion, he swept to the floor, his long, black coat billowing out behind him. I heard gasps from all around. He was on one knee, with a ring from a cracker in his hand and the other still clasping mine.

I giggled. I couldn't help it. I had dreamt of diamond rings, not plastic pink ones. His eyes started to cloud over and there was a tightness to his lips.

"I want you to marry me," he said, his grip gaining in strength.

"No," I said, barely thinking about my words, "I don't love you. I don't want to marry you."

His head tipped back and his mouth gaped open. A scream shot out. Then he hauled himself up, his hand releasing mine. His face flushed red, then deathly white. I heard screams again, though they weren't from him this time. I looked round. Everyone was backing away.

"Lesley! Run!" someone shouted.

Then I saw the gun – too late. He leapt at me, grabbing my arm and dragging me towards the staff room. Only Daniel was in there, the head librarian. He saw me and started to smile. It swiftly slid off his face when he saw the gun and who was holding it.

For a moment, I thought Daniel was going to run at him, to knock him to the ground and grab the gun. I shook my head. What if it didn't happen that way? What if Daniel slipped and was killed? I closed my eyes. I couldn't bear it. So Daniel went free and the door closed upon us.

There has been lots of noise and movement outside the door. Daniel will have called the police. Staff will have been moved to safety.

All because of me. For a love that can never be. I can feel a tear trickling down my cheek. I should hate the man in front of me. But I can't. I know how he feels. I know what it's like to love someone and not to have that love returned. To feel your heart being torn in two when they ask someone else to dance with them at the Christmas do. To look longingly at them each and every day and to know that they barely see you.

"It's him, isn't it? That head library man."

My head shoots up at his words, the first words he has uttered since his proposal. The gun is pointing at me. My eyes fly from the gun to his cold, piercing ones. I start to cry, shivering and shaking uncontrollably. Despite everything, I didn't think he would kill me. But then, I realise I don't know what I thought he was going to do.

His next actions surprise me. The coldness is gone, replaced by that softness, that gentleness and kindness. Now, it is he who is crying, shivering and shaking as if he will never stop. The gun falls to the floor. My eyes follow it. It's a toy. A little boy's toy.

I think about running to the door and yanking it open. To freedom. The police will be waiting. They'll usher me to safety and then they'll get him. But they don't know it's a toy gun. Perhaps they will be armed. Maybe he'll run and they'll take him down.

"What's your name?" I have to know.

"Kevin. I just wanted to marry you," he says.

"I know. But you're right. It is Daniel, the head librarian. I've been in love with him for as long as I can remember. He doesn't love me, but I can't stop loving him. I'm sorry," I say.

"I've been in love with you for as long as I can remember. You don't love me, but I can't stop loving you," he whispers.

I lean forward, hardly able to hear him.

"Go," he says, nodding towards the door.

I look at him. I'll tell the police it's a toy, that they mustn't hurt him and that he didn't mean it.

"I'm sorry," he says.

I place my hand on his arm. I move on and open the door, the tears streaming down my face. I do everything I promised myself, but it won't make any difference. I can hear them slamming him to the floor, hear them reading him his rights and slapping the handcuffs on him.

It seems to take forever to get to the main door.

"Your boyfriend is waiting for you. He's been pacing up and down the whole time. I'd keep hold of that one if I were you," a policewoman says, holding the door open for me.

"I haven't got a boyfriend," I say.

"Well, someone's very much in love with you," she says.

Then I see him. Daniel. He is striding up and down, clenching his fists. He stops, puts one fist into his mouth and bites down onto it. It drops to his side and he starts to stride up and down again. He stops and turns towards me. He looks at me longingly. Why hasn't he done that before? Perhaps he has. Maybe he thought I was the one who barely knew he was there. Why didn't he ask me to dance? Perhaps he thought I would reject him.

Suddenly he is running towards me. His arms wrap round me, holding me close, his breath soft on my ear. I hope he never lets me go.

I see Kevin being bundled into the police car. But it isn't the man I see. I see that boy at the back. I look harder. I can't see that little girl anymore. She's gone, but the little boy will always be there.

The Intruder

"Shoo. Go on, get out of it," Trevor said, lashing out with his leg.

The cat whimpered, staring up at him with huge, sorrowful eyes. Trevor sighed. He shouldn't have kicked the thing. Well, he hadn't really. There hadn't been much oomph in that kick. In fact, it had been more of a nudge.

"Don't you have somewhere to go?" Trevor asked, watching the black nose wrinkle, sniffing and savouring the sumptuous smell hanging in the air.

Trevor hugged his fish and chips close. He didn't care how hungry she was or how pitiful she could make herself look. She wasn't getting any of his fish and chips and that was that.

Trevor picked out a particularly succulent looking chip. He opened his mouth and popped it in. He meant to take his time, to feel the food in his mouth. But he couldn't. In two chomps, it was gone. Then he pushed another into his mouth and another.

He hadn't been able to believe it when the young woman had thrown them in the waste-paper bin, wrinkling her nose in distaste.

Trevor hadn't hesitated. It wasn't often he had a whole fish and chip supper to himself.

"Meow."

"You still here?" Trevor said, "you don't give up, do you?"

She reached up a paw. She was brave. He had to grant her that. Trevor pursed his lips. A little bit of fish wouldn't hurt. He looked at the thin layer of fur barely hiding bones. He frowned, seeing the cuts covering her and the whiskers, worn and withered.

"You're a bit like me, aren't you?" he said, thinking about his shabby coat and shaggy hair.

He threw some fish to the ground. The cat pounced on it, greedily gulping it. He wondered if she'd ever known the love of a home, like the loving home he'd once had, full of warmth and kindness. Trevor felt a tear prod at the back of his eyes. It had been ten years since Nancy and little Katie died. It still made him want to cry.

But he had been happy. At least he had those memories to take him through those endless dark nights when winter showed her chill. He could close his eyes and the image of a Christmas tree by a dazzling fire came to mind. Nancy was there and Katie, too. He smiled, seeing the joy on Katie's face as she tore open a parcel to reveal a wondrous surprise. His smile grew wider as he took in the love and elation reflected in Nancy's face.

Yes, he had those memories. The other ones were fading now. The ones of the crash – of faces contorted in pain, of cries as the car careered into the ditch. Then darkness and the awakening to find he was the only one left alive.

He shuddered, banishing the images. He screwed up the fish and chip paper and placed it in the bin.

"What am I going to call you?" he said, turning to the cat. "Well, that's just great. Now you've had your feed, you don't need me anymore, do you?"

He shook his head. What did it matter if she was gone? He didn't like cats anyway.

But later that night, he felt a brush of something against his leg. Trevor pulled the blanket tightly round his chin. When she realised there wasn't anything to eat, she'd be off. He probably wouldn't see her again. He sniffed. Not that it mattered, because he really didn't like cats.

When he awoke the next morning to a dull and dark day, he was surprised to feel a lump by his leg. He peeked over the blanket and there she was, curled up as small as small could be.

He was going to call her Kitty. She wasn't a kitten, he knew that much, but she was as small as one. Yes, Kitty would do. He wasn't going to go wasting time thinking up extravagant names for a cat he didn't even like.

Suddenly the tiny bundle came alive, springing up and scurrying across the path. Two seconds later, she returned triumphantly holding a mouse between her teeth. She plopped it on the blanket and meowed proudly.

"No thanks, you have it," Trevor said, feeling rather green and walking away.

Trevor turned. He could hear cries. Kitty.

He ran forward, his breaths catching in his throat.

They were only young boys, but there were so many of them. Kicking. Prodding. Poking. He felt angry. So very angry, like nothing he'd ever felt before. His arms

17

flew out and a great grunt grew up from inside him. He opened his mouth and unleashed it, racing towards the boys all the while.

"Quick, let's go," one boy yelled.

And then they were gone, their taunts and jeers with them.

The tears came this time. He was too late. She was dead. He reached out his hand and rested it on her still-warm body. He closed his eyes and thought about Nancy and Katie. They would have liked Kitty. Katie always wanted a kitten. But he'd always said no.

Trevor gulped back another flurry of tears. He hadn't even known her for a day. But she had been the first friend he'd had in years.

He would have to move on now. Those boys would probably be back, with their parents, too or the police. Before he went, he would bury her, put her somewhere special.

He opened his eyes and moved to pick her up. He stopped. Two eyes were looking at him. He was sure they had been shut before. He looked at her chest. Up and down it went.

"Kitty," he cried, bending to hug her.

"Meow," she said, weakly.

"Sorry, Kitty," he said, moving back, "I'll look after you. I'll nurse you. You'll be all right with me."

Trevor looked at Kitty and she looked back at him. He was sure she smiled. He smiled, too. Trevor, who now rather liked cats.

Joshua's Will

There would be no reading of the last will and testament of Joshua Needham.

The mourners gathered around the coffin, their umbrellas held high against the bitter and driving November rain. Some wept unashamedly, others coughed into their handkerchiefs and many turned away, unable to deal with the cruelty of life.

Gayle squeezed David's hand, her tear-streaked face a permanent fixture over the past eleven days. She watched, still disbelieving as the casket was lowered into the gaping hole.

"Oh, David. Why us? Why our little boy? He was only eight years old. I can't bear it. I can't!" Gayle collapsed against him.

David wrapped his arms around her, battling for a strength he didn't feel. His eyes searched the sea of faces filling the churchyard. Many were strangers, well-wishers who felt a sadness for the child he had lost. For a moment, he wished it were one of them standing in his shoes, grieving for the loss of their only child. He swallowed, a fight against the growing lump in his throat. He didn't mean it. No one should ever have to feel the hurt he was going through. It clawed at him, reminding him every instant of every day.

A light in the distance caught his eye. His head jerked up. A smile slowly spread over his features, restoring him momentarily to the handsome man he was.

Joshua stood between the trees, the huge oak and the fir tree in the corner. His blond hair shone and his dark eyes sparkled, his grin growing wider. His legs were clad in denim jeans moving faster and faster, almost stumbling as he ran towards his father. David couldn't move. His smile faded. Joshua was lost amongst the throng of people. David found his feet, leaving Gayle to fend for herself, his gaze focusing on a flash of blue.

"Joshua! Joshua! It's Daddy. Come on. I'm here, Joshua," his shouts were frantic.

*

Gayle thanked the doctor and closed the front door. She fell against it, glad the day was almost over. Mechanically, her legs carried her into the lounge. Her heart reached out to David, sedated and dozing in the chair. She gently shut the door and made her way upstairs.

She paused, fingering the doorknob and stared at the nameplate dangling from the single screw. She smiled, remembering a prior conversation.

"I'm too old for that stupid thing. Can't you take it down, Mum?"

"But it's lovely. Granny bought you that. You loved the teddies spelling out your name."

Gayle knew it would remain on his door forever.

Slowly, she turned the handle, her mind telling her no, that she wasn't ready, but her hands took on a life of their own.

The familiar dark shapes revealed themselves as she turned on the light. Her whole body ached, memories flooding into her head. She walked over to the bed, the sheets crumpled and worn. She stared at the imprint of his frail body and gently stroked the indent. Sinking down beside the bed, she drank in his familiar scent; a combination of his father's favourite aftershave and smelly football boots.

Her eyes spilled over with tears. She looked up, her eyes coming to rest on the shelf. The photograph of the three of them on Joshua's seventh birthday stood proudly, smiles beaming out, blissfully unaware of the horrors to come. In hindsight, she should have known. She could see it now, his gaunt face, the thin frame and dark circles under his eyes. It was all there in the picture.

But not cancer. He shouldn't have had cancer. He was too young for suffering and certainly too young to die.

She stared up at the Manchester United strip hanging on the back of his door. All Joshua had ever wanted was to play for their team. And he would have one day. All his teachers thought he would give Wayne Rooney a run for his money. But it was too late. He would never kick a football again.

Nor would he ever reopen his school bag. The pages of his exercise books would remain unfilled, his chair at school soon to be taken by another pupil. His friends were shocked and upset. They shouldn't have to see one of their friends die. They should all have grown old together, gone to college and out to parties. His friends would, but Joshua wouldn't. He would always remain an eight-year-old boy. Eight years, six months and two days. He would never grow a day older.

Gayle sank down onto the floor, her cry raw and ragged. She gagged, unable to control the sickness in her stomach. Her hands clawed at the soft, blue carpet. The room spun. Images blurred. She was losing it. Her eyes tried to focus. The colours whizzed by to be replaced by darkness.

*

She awoke, her eyes staring up at the naked bulb, its light blinding her for an instant. They had meant to replace the old Peter Rabbit shade with his favourite football team. Maybe she would buy one. He would like that.

The television, the highlight of his small room, drew her to it. An envelope leant against it. The words, 'Mum and Dad' were a stark reminder that he was no longer there. She grabbed the white paper, imagining his smaller fingers touching it. She held it to her cheek, savouring it.

*

"Gayle?" David's voice was urgent.

"I'm up here," her voice was a croak.

She heard his heavy footsteps on the stairs and the door swung open. His face, etched in pain, peered round the door. He staggered into the room and Gayle took him in her arms as he collapsed against her.

"Maybe we'll open the envelope another day," Gayle said through her tears.

"What envelope?"

"This one. It's...it's from Joshua."

David took it from her. His finger hovered over the flap before tearing it open. A DVD dropped to the floor. Their gazes were rigid upon it, each hardly daring to breathe.

David switched the TV on, inserted the DVD and pressed play. He sank back against the bed, not sure if he could bear to watch.

Joshua's smiling image filled the screen and his voice, confident and happy, rang out.

"This is the last will and testament of Joshua James Needham of sixty-three, Saint Bernard's Close, Chorlewood, CH12 9LY. Anyway, I hope this is ok. I found your will in the drawer. I didn't look at it, honest. But I thought I'd better do mine, seeing as I'm going soon.

"I know you'll probably cry when you see this. I heard you both when you thought I was asleep. Please don't be sad. I'm not. I'm going up to heaven. The angels will look after me. I'll be able to eat chocolate cake every day and you won't be able to tell me off for eating it.

"I know I'll have lots of other children to play with. We'll be able to run around and maybe I'll make the football team. And I'm sure I'll meet all those famous footballers who are up there, too. I might even beat them.

"Anyway, onto this will stuff. First of all, I leave my big Ted to you, Mum. He'll protect you and look after you when you're sad. He always saved me from the monsters in the cupboard at night and when I was in hospital. To Dad, I leave my little Ted, because Dad's big and strong and doesn't need the big Ted, but every now and then you need a friend. Little Ted always watched over my bedside cabinet.

"To my friend, Oliver, I leave all my remote control cars. I know he's always wanted them and they're so much better than his.

"I want to give...um, I suppose Katie is my girlfriend, but we didn't kiss or anything like that. I'm not a sissy, but she was quite nice. I want to give her all my other teddy bears. I was too old for them anyway. And she collects them, as well as silly dolls.

"I did think about giving my best friend, Sam, all my football stuff, but I can't. I'd like that to go to my little brother, with the rest of my stuff.

"I know, you're asking, 'what little brother?' I don't know why, but I just know I'm going to have a little brother in the future. It's a shame I won't meet him, though I'm sure the angels will let me have a peek at him. And I'm sure I'll be allowed to come and see you every once in a while.

"I suppose that's it. Oh, I almost forgot. Sam will want something. He can have my money box. There's nearly twenty pounds in it. He's been saving up for a laptop for ages, so my money can go towards it.

"Well, there's nothing else I want to give, except my love to you. As parents go, you two have been the best. I'll always love you. Please don't be sad. I'll be with you every day, somewhere and I know I'll always be with you in your hearts.

"Goodbye, Mum and Dad. I love you."

Tears streamed down their faces. Gayle and David smiled at one another, their first smile in almost two weeks.

Complaining

From: A.moaner@expectationshigh.co.uk
To: I.M.shoddy@imgoodfornothing.com

Dear Mr Shoddy,
It is with the utmost regret that I have to send you this e-mail. My regret however, is not for you, but for the sheer torment and torture my wife and I have endured whilst staying at your guesthouse, 'Homeleigh', though why it should have been named as such is beyond me. Perhaps residents who live in a cesspit would find it 'homeleigh', but my wife and I certainly did not.

I can see why you reside in Spain, no doubt in an expensive, exotic villa, whilst your minions attempt to hold the place over here together.

I shan't take up too much of your precious sunbathing and relaxing time, but my complaints are as follows:

1. Whilst I am of a mature age and have been through the 1970s in terms of style and dress, thirty years have since passed and turquoise and brown décor are not what I would expect of

a 'top' guesthouse, as advertised in 'Guesthouse Weekly.' It would also seem that collecting is the hotel's creed judging by the collection of dust, litter etc on display. I am sure all the rooms have not been cleaned since the 1970s either.

2. On seeing the chambermaid, I did reach an understanding of why the rooms are in their current state. Doris was very proud in her telling me about the 90th birthday party her son is holding for her next year. However she is worried about what will happen to the rooms when she goes into hospital for surgery soon. She wouldn't tell me what the surgery was for, but judging by her stooped spine, gammy leg, arthritic hands and her inability to see anything further than a foot away, it could be for anything. May I suggest you retire her and find a suitable replacement? Someone under the age of 90 would be preferable.

3. I presume the pigeon perching on the bath taps had mistakenly entered the guesthouse through an open window and is not something you provide as an extra for all your guests. My wife was most upset when the said pigeon flew round the room three times before proceeding to relieve himself on top of her head. She had to use all her spare shampoo to get the vile substance out and unfortunately your guest house, not being of the standard we are used to, does not provide shampoo, soap, shower

gel, toilet roll or in fact anything to do with cleanliness.

4. I would also like to point out that as you seem able to afford a villa in Spain, then I am sure you could afford new beds for the rooms. Using breezeblocks to hold them up is not acceptable. My wife, being rather fond of her food and a little on the large side, climbed carefully into the bed and received a dreadful fright when it collapsed.

5. Nevertheless, I would consider recommending your guesthouse to people who wish to lose a vast amount of weight in a very short space of time. Sickness and dysentery are guaranteed as a result of even inhaling the slightest scent of the substances being cooked up in the kitchen. As for the food itself, well that's another matter. Whilst serving with the army all over the world and being exposed to all manner of situations, I didn't ever have the misfortune of tasting such atrocious food. Manure would taste better.

I could go on with my complaints, but it is too distressing to recall all the unfortunate incidents, which have taken place during our stay. I thought it only polite to address you before taking the matter further and seeking compensation.

Yours grudgingly,
Mr. Moaner (A.)

From: I.M.shoddy@imgoodfornothing.com
To: A.moaner@expectationshigh.co.uk

Dear Mr Moaner,

I was delighted to receive your e-mail. I was having a well-earned break from the glorious sunshine and sipping champagne from my finest, crystal glasses when I received it.

I am so sorry that you did not enjoy your stay at 'Homeleigh.' I run a chain of 'Homeleigh' guesthouses all over the country and all of my guests express absolute joy in staying in them. Though, as you so kindly point out, as they usually live in cesspits they feel right at home.

I shall now look at each of your complaints in turn and I sincerely hope to resolve them:

1. It is the distinctive style of our rooms that so many of our guests enjoy. I have had numerous requests for the rooms to remain exactly as they are and of course as the guests are my most important concern, I have chosen to grant them their wish. The issue of dust is dealt with in the next point.

2. I am so glad you enjoyed meeting Mother. She is a wondrous lady and she has always looked after our No. 1 'Homeleigh' guesthouse, which of course is the one you and your lovely lady wife stayed in. Mother refuses to retire and, as many of our guests have written in the guest book, 'the place wouldn't be the same without her.' Her

surgery incidentally is for a breast enlargement.

3. I have considered charging you extra for the pigeon, but as a gesture of goodwill, I shall not be. We do not provide shampoo, soap, shower gel or toilet roll because our guests, used to living in cesspits, do not require them.

4. The breezeblock beds are a new design and as we have not had any ladies who perhaps enjoy their food as much as your lovely lady wife, then the collapsing of them has not been an issue. Maybe it will no longer be a problem for your wife due to point 5 below.

5. How kind of you to consider recommending my guesthouse as a way of losing weight. I hope your wife took up this service. What a fantastic idea. I shall be considering it forthwith. And as for the food, it is of course manure, which is in keeping with the diet of those living in cesspits.

I note that in your e-mail you have more issues to discuss. I wonder if they relate to our renowned entertainment. I would be most grateful if you could inform me of these further issues. I do so want to make everything right for such valued guests as yourselves. I thoroughly look forward to hearing from you.

I regret that I must now head off for my six-course supper.

Fondest regards,
I.M. Shoddy

From: A.moaner@expectationshigh.co.uk
To: I.M.shoddy@imgoodfornothing.com

Dear Mr Shoddy,
I am outraged by the tone of your e-mail. It has caused even further trauma to my wife, especially with your mention of entertainment. Pole-dancing lessons do not constitute our idea of entertainment. I cannot be drawn into further discussion of it.

I have nothing more to write and you will be hearing from my solicitor in the very immediate future.

Yours extremely grudgingly,
Mr. Moaner (A.)

From: I.M.shoddy@imgoodfornothing.com
To: A.moaner@expectationshigh.co.uk

Dear Mr Moaner,

Once again, your e-mail reaches me as I take a break, though this time from mansion hunting. I am currently looking for something a little bigger than my ten-bed roomed villa, with three bathrooms, two swimming pools, tennis court, jacuzzi, sauna and three acres of land.

I digress. On to your e-mail. I am surprised to read that you are a man who likes up-to-date décor and yet one who does not like up-to-date entertainment. Pole dancing is the latest fashion. It would also help your wife to tone up her 'little on the large size' as you put it. I also offer such entertainment free, included in the price of your stay, which you won't find anywhere else.

I hope you will change your mind about contacting your solicitor. It would be an awful shame to put Mother out of work and onto the streets.

Fondest regards once again,
I.M. Shoddy

From: A.moaner@expectationshigh.co.uk
To: I.M.shoddy@imgoodfornothing.com

Dear Mr Shoddy,

Now it is my turn to be delighted to write to you. My solicitor has informed me that all the 'Homeleigh' guesthouses have been closed down. Apparently they have been under investigation for some time. Doris has taken a job as our live-in housekeeper (light duties only) and I do believe she is having the time of her life. We have also managed to persuade her that she doesn't need the surgery.

I am enthralled to hear that you have also been under investigation for various misdemeanours. As you read this, you will no doubt be hearing a very big knock on your door and the rattle of handcuffs. I do hope you enjoy prison, but please be rest assured that your mother will be well cared for. We are taking her on holiday with us on a round-the-world cruise in place of her 90th birthday party, which I am sorry to say you will miss. We will give her an extra special card on your behalf.

With *my* fondest regards,
Mr Moaner (A.)

Two in the Morning

I had the greatest gift of all. Now it's gone. And it can't ever come back.

I loved Megan as soon as I saw her. She was beautiful – to me anyway.

"What's that supposed to be?" my husband, Jez said, poking at what was obviously a cute button nose.

"And that's a leg, is it?" he continued, turning the scan picture this way and then that. He screwed up his nose. "Doesn't look much like a baby."

I just shook my head. Of course she looked like a baby. A perfect baby. My baby.

I couldn't wait to feel her first kick. She was very good at it, too, especially at two in the morning. But that made sense afterwards. Two in the morning was always one of her feeding times. That was our special time. Two in the morning, I'd hear her cries, so soft, so sweet at first, then she'd open that tiny mouth wide and a piercing wail would be unleashed, gaining momentum with each second it took me to reach her.

I would look at Jez as I lifted her out of her Moses basket and took her downstairs. His eyes were always firmly closed, his arms and legs splayed out in the sleep only men seem to have the luxury of. Then I would close the door and we would go downstairs. It was our time. Just the two of us.

I look at my watch. Two in the morning. Our time. Just the two of us. But she's not here. I close my eyes, wanting to picture her, but already she's fading from me. I don't want her to go. I want to cherish her for eternity. I want her image in my mind forever. Every silky hair on her head, every mark on that baby face, every movement of those rosebud lips. I've got photographs. Hundreds of photographs. But that's not enough.

I can feel tears tumbling down my cheeks. It hurts. But it isn't the tears that hurt. I lost my parents when I was four. I can't remember how that felt. I must have been sad, so very, very sad. Yet children see things differently. They cope. They get on with life. Not like adults. I'm sure I didn't feel pain then. Not the sharp, raw pain of a love lost.

I think about the moment when I wasn't sure I would love her. How could I have thought that for even one moment? But I did. My waters had just broken. I looked at my watch. It was two in the morning. I lay there a while – in the dark and terrified. I had read all the books, been to all the classes and suddenly I was scared. What if Megan didn't love me? What if I wasn't a good mum? For a moment, just that one moment, I wanted to run away from it all.

Jez saved me. I thought he would be the one to go to pieces, to fumble and not know what to do. He took it all in his stride. He told me how wonderful I was, how he loved me and how we would be the best parents in the world. He held my hand as I screeched and screamed my way through labour.

"They can see her head," Jez said, not moving from my side, "this is it, Carrie."

I saw the love in his eyes, the tears and I knew, even before I saw her. I knew I loved her. And she me. It would take time and it did, but I knew I would be a good mum. I cried so much the day she was born. Tears of joy, pure joy, like nothing I had ever felt before. Just like these tears, yesterday's tears and all the days before that are unlike anything I've felt before.

I thought the pain would ease. But how can the pain of losing the greatest gift of all ease? Jez has been the strong one. He organized the funeral, thanked everyone for their support and held me tightly as I fell apart. He had to be strong. But he isn't. Not really. I've seen the way he looks at her picture and the way he strokes her baby grows before touching them to his cheek. I've heard him cry himself to sleep at night and watched him stare at the TV screen, his mind with Megan.

I remember the day she died so clearly. She rolled over. All by herself. I was so proud. She looked up at me with those big, blue eyes, wondering what all the fuss was about as I clapped and cheered. The rest of the day was spent washing, changing nappies, warming bottles, putting her down for sleeps and dashing round doing chores in between. A normal day, aside from that one magical moment. But then every moment with Megan was magical.

The next day she was dead. We didn't even have

a chance to say goodbye. I woke up. It was nearer three than two in the morning. I knew something was wrong. There were no soft, sweet cries, no piercing wails. I leapt out of bed and I went to her. She was so silent, so still. I didn't believe it at first. I didn't want to. The words 'cot death' rang through my mind. Then wails did fill the air, but not her wails – mine.

It wasn't 'cot death'. It was her heart. She had a problem no one could have known about. She had a one in a million chance of having such a condition. I hadn't wanted to hear the words. I had pounded my fists, hitting out at the doctor when he told me. Jez led me away. Then I turned to him, pounding at his chest and sobbing until I had nothing left.

How I wished we'd had one last night together. One last two in the morning. I could have told her I loved her, that I'd always remember her and that no one could ever take her place. But if I'd known that she was to be taken from me, I'd have clung to her, watching her every movement, knowing that any moment could be her last.

Each new day would have been worse than the one before, bringing her closer to death. I couldn't have done that. I couldn't have watched her slip away.

It's been a year since Megan died. I don't think I've missed my nightly vigil once, not since that last night. I did wonder if I had woken that night at two, instead of nearer three, I could have saved her. The doctors said I would have been too late anyway.

I look at my watch. Half past two now. Megan always took half an hour to feed. Then I would kiss and cuddle her, telling her over and over that I loved her before we began our journey up the stairs and back to bed.

I start that same journey, my arms empty this time. I can hear Jez's snores gaining momentum with each step I take. It was a long time before we talked about having another baby. It was me who brought it up.

"I can't ever replace, Megan," I blurted out to him one evening.

I didn't know where that had come from. It was something I had refused to let myself think about. And once I thought about it, I felt so guilty as if I had betrayed her. Jez hadn't taken his eyes from the flickering screen, oblivious to my words, as he replayed a memory with Megan in his mind. It didn't matter anyway. Neither of us could ever think about replacing her. I went to leave the room.

"I know," he said.

I looked back at him. He came to my side and stroked my face.

"I don't think I could, either. She was special. Our Megan."

And then he kissed me. Such tenderness. In life Megan had brought us closer together and in death, closer still.

I knew I was pregnant straight away. I felt different. The morning sickness soon kicked in, which confirmed it. I thought I would be horrified. Ashamedly, I thought I would want the child wrenched from me. It wasn't Megan. It could never be Megan. I didn't want it.

But I did. I loved that child growing inside me. He or she wasn't Megan and I knew they could never replace her. But I had to have this child. I had to protect him or her. Megan would have wanted me to.

I didn't know how to tell Jez. It was different for me. Motherly instinct, emotions, whatever it was, was taking over. It wouldn't be the same for him. In the end, I didn't need to say a word.

"You're pregnant, aren't you?" he said, one morning after I tried to tip the cup of tea he'd made me down the sink without him seeing.

I hadn't been able to stomach tea or coffee when I had been carrying Megan, either.

I had stayed there at the sink for a long while, not wanting to see his face, to see the horror reflected in his eyes. Would he think I had planned it? Would he think that I could replace our little girl, just like that?

I felt his arms around me. He pulled me to face him and he looked into my eyes. Then he smiled.

I look at him now, with his head poking out the duvet and hair sticking up all over the place. I pat my stomach. It's a boy this time. I'm sure of it. A baby brother for Megan. We'll tell him all about his sister. He would have loved her. And Megan him. I don't think he'll be a two in the morning baby. That's just for me and Megan.

It still hurts, so very, very much and always will. But we've been given a second gift – that most precious gift of all – love.

The Best and Worst Bonfire Night Ever

Tom

I hate Mum. I hate Dad and I hate Felicity. It's bonfire night and I hate bonfire night. We've been standing in the middle of a stupid field for half an hour and we've not even heard one single bang or seen anything, which could be called a flash. I didn't want to come anyway. Felicity did. She clapped her hands and got all excited when Mum and Dad started talking about fireworks. But she claps her hands and gets excited about everything. It's what girls do.

Edgar

I still can't believe how silly people can be. I mean, leaving your door unlocked is just asking for trouble, isn't it? Especially on bonfire night. Everyone is out and it's an open invitation for a burglar.

This house isn't bad. Not the one I had in mind – they did lock their door, but I'm getting on a bit and you've got to make life easier for yourself. Besides, it'll do.

It's a shame that firework displays aren't on for longer. I could do the whole street then.

Tom

Felicity is starting to get bored now. I knew she would. She'll hate the fireworks, too. She'll cry and scream. All girls cry and scream.

Edgar

There's someone in the house. I can hear heavy breathing. I've never made that mistake before. I need to retire. I've been doing this job too long. But who can it be? I saw them go off – the four of them: the mum and dad, all excited and grinning like teenagers with a sordid secret, the sulky lad and wailing girl. The breathing has stopped now. Perhaps I'm imagining things. I'm definitely too old for this. There it is again. Closer now.

Tom

I knew it. I told them. But they didn't listen. They never listen. There have only been a couple of pathetic whizzes and one whoosh and Felicity is going bananas. Dad's passing her to Mum now. He always does that. As long as I don't get her, I don't care. She's all sticky and gooey and she pulls my hair. She smells a lot, too.

Edgar

It's a cat. A bloomin' cat. I've never heard a cat snore before. He's quite cute really. He looks a bit Persian, with a squashed up nose and he's got a lovely tail.

What on earth is wrong with me? Last month I got

all sentimental over a poor goldfish in a tiny tank. Poor thing had obviously been lying on its side for a while. But I shouldn't even be looking. I should be in, up those stairs and into the jewellery box and out again in the blink of an eye.

Tom

Yes, yes, yes! We're going home. I actually feel quite sorry for Felicity (though I wouldn't want everyone to know that). She's got herself in a right state. I thought she was going to be sick. Thank goodness she hasn't been. Her sick is horrible and it goes everywhere.

Mum and Dad look very cheesed off. I'm not surprised at a fiver a time. And it's nearly over already.

Edgar

Quickly does it. That's it. I'm motoring now – up the stairs and ow! My foot. It's broken. I wish my torch was more powerful, but being a professional like I am, I can't risk it. I can't have everyone seeing that circle of light. Still, I wouldn't mind seeing what I trod on. There it is – a horse. A plastic horse.

Tom

I don't believe it. We've almost made it to the gate and someone's yelling at us. Oh no. It's Aunty Jane. She's running towards us. She's going to do it, isn't she? Ugh! Why does she have to kiss me? And she always wears florescent pink lipstick, which seems to stay on my cheek forever. She ruffles my hair, too. She ruins it. I wouldn't have bothered with the gel if I'd known.

I can see Dave McGregor from school over there. He's watching me and lapping all this up. It'll be all round school by Monday afternoon. It's not fair.

Edgar
I've made it. Finally. Over crying dolls, squeaking clowns and metal cars. The jewellery had better be worth it.

There we go. This is the room. I've an eye for this sort of thing. Though, it is the only room with a nice white door and no stickers, posters or scribble covering it. Still, you never know these days.

I can't believe it. This family may as well have written, 'Come in all burglars. Take what you like,' on the front door. There are rings, necklaces, and bracelets – all spilling out of the open jewellery box.

Look at that. There's a photo right beside the box. A great big one. Can't miss it. They look a really nice family, actually. The wife's a bit of a stunner. She looks half my age. But then she probably is. The bloke looks a bit smarmy. The city-businessman sort. The lad doesn't look so sullen in the photo. He's got a great smile. He'll be a real looker and have all the girls swooning over him in a few years' time. The little girl's a cutie. Look at those dimples. It makes you want to tickle her under the chin.

For goodness sake. Get a grip, Edgar. I've never cared about them before. Blimey, I couldn't begin to count the amount of people I've robbed over the years. I've done quite well for myself really. Though, not so well that I could have retired before my 65th birthday.

And I should have done. I almost did last week. But it's the wife. She wants a ruby ring for our anniversary.

I've been searching for the right one for ages now. I thought I had found the perfect one last week. But it was a fake – just a bit of red glass. I couldn't see in the torchlight, but I had my suspicions. Not everyone would know, but I've an eye for these sort of things.

There's a lovely lot to choose from here. And a ruby ring. A real beauty. I should just take the ring, but I'll really be in the wife's good books if I take this bracelet to go with it. She'll love this necklace, too.

Tom

Thank goodness we got away. I'm sure Aunty Jane lies in a bath of cheap perfume every morning. I thought I was going to choke.

At least it isn't far to go home. I think I'll run on ahead. Mum and Dad are going on and on about how lovely Aunty Jane is and how much weight she has lost. Perhaps it's her coat. She still looks like a great big teddy bear with clown make-up on to me.

Edgar

Right. Just the ring, bracelet and necklace it is then. It's such a shame to leave all that lovely loot lying there. Maybe I'll just take that pair of pearl earrings as well. The wife loves pearls. She's got a pearl necklace. Probably got about ten of them, but no earrings.

I don't believe it. I can feel their eyes on me – all of them, staring out of their photo. I wish they would stop it. They can spare a bit of jewellery. What's a little old ruby ring to them? If it was that precious, it would be on a finger, wouldn't it? But what if it belonged to a dear, beloved grandma? They'll be so upset to lose it.

Right, that's it. I'm retiring. I can't stand much more of this. It's doing my head in. I'm taking the ring, necklace and bracelet. The wife can do without the pearls.

I'd better get down those stairs quickly. I've been here far too long. I don't think I've heard a bang for a while now. I'd better get off before they come back. That really wouldn't do.

Tom

I'm almost at the corner now. I can hear Dad calling me. He thinks I'm still five-years-old. I can see our house now. It's a shame I haven't got a key. Then I could go up to my room and get on the PS3 and my favourite racing car game. I don't think Mum and Dad will ever let me have a key. Perhaps when I'm thirty and I'll have left home long before then.

But I would be better than them at locking the door and looking after the keys. Dad's always locking himself out and Mum sticks them in the front door and forgets to take them out. She spends hours looking for them and I always get the blame.

Edgar

That damn plastic horse nearly got me again. That's it, down the last stair safely. I should feel relieved it's all over. But I feel a bit tearful actually. No more planning, no more trying doors and windows. I'll miss old Arthur, too. He buys all my stuff. Perhaps we can meet up now and then. Have a cup of tea and a chat.

I've got to go, get out of here before I break down

and cry my eyes out. Lift the handle, easy does it, slip out the door and hurry home.

Tom

I might as well go on up to the door. Mum might have forgotten to lock it. She does that sometimes, too. Then I can be round Silverstone before they've even reached the end of the drive. I think I'll be Sebastian Vettel today, speeding up the straight at over 200mph. Uh oh. Bumphh!

Edgar

Bumphh! Who's that? Now I'm sat on my bottom. It doesn't half hurt. I don't think I can get up.

Tom

Who on earth is that? He really hurt my arm. That's Mum's jewellery all over the ground. He's been in our house. He's a burglar. A real live burglar. What am I going to do?

Now Dad is behind me. He's looking at me, now at the man and onto the jewellery and back to me again.

He's telling me how well I've done. Now he's reaching for his mobile phone. He says he's ringing the police. Wow! The police. There will be sirens wailing and lights flashing. I stopped him. I stopped the burglar. I did it. It'll be all round school by Monday afternoon. Cool. This is the best bonfire night ever.

Edgar

I knew I should have retired last week. This is the worst bonfire night ever.

Bubbles

———

"What on earth are you doing to Bubbles, Adam?" Mary said, watching as her seven-year-old son poked and prodded the brilliant orange fish.

She marched over to the tank and extracted the magician's wand from grubby fingers.

"Don't ever let me see you do that again. Poor Bubbles," Mary said, putting the offending weapon on top of the highest shelf.

"I wasn't. I didn't...I only poked him 'cos he wasn't moving. Look, Mum, look," Adam said, his face flushing poppy red to pansy purple.

Mary looked into the murky depths and made a mental note to clean the tank more often. Dear Bubbles. He loved gliding through the water and fancifully flicking his tail as a fish flake caught his eye. He had been so pleased, if fish could ever be pleased, when Adam had chosen an archway for him to dart in and out of. Mary sighed as she stared at the bloated body bobbing on top of the water.

"He's dead, isn't he? Everything dies. First Grandad died. Then Daddy died. And now Bubbles. I loved Bubbles.

He was…he was my friend," Adam said and his pale blue eyes welled up.

Mary found herself blinking away her own tears as she pulled Adam to her. She patted his back, soothing him as his body shook with sobs. Adam was right. Everything died. It was two years since her own father had passed away. Adam had loved his Grandad Ted. Grandad Ted had taken him to the park, taught him how to ride a tricycle and kick a football. He had been a fantastic father to Mary, too and he always had time for children.

Her husband, Jim, had been just the same. They always said daughters married someone like their father. Perhaps they were right. Jim had helped them both cope without Grandad Ted. Then the cancer had come, cruelly spreading and seizing Jim's life not long after. And now death had come to claim another. Life could be so unfair.

Mary felt her chest tighten. Adam had suffered so much already. It had taken a lot for him to trust and love again. Even if that love was for a fish. She remembered when her sister had knocked on the door a few weeks after Jim's funeral.

"I thought Adam might like this," Nancy said, dangling Bubbles under Mary's nose, "might help the boy forget about his dad."

Mary had never gotten on with her older sister and at that moment, she had fought against her initial instinct to slam the door in her face. Instead, she had chosen to rescue poor Bubbles who was turning a very pale orange as Nancy swung him to and fro.

Mary wondered if she had acted wisely when Adam first set eyes on Bubbles.

"I don't want a stupid fish. I want my daddy back," he had said, stomping up to his room.

Mary had persevered and bought a tank, a very large tank after listening to the 'helpful' salesman. Poor Bubbles looked lost in his new home, so stones and plant life had gradually been added.

"What do I want a fish for? They don't do anything," Adam pouted, refusing to have anything to do with Bubbles.

Though as each day passed, Mary would watch from the kitchen as Adam stopped by the tank with a small smile on his face and talked to Bubbles.

"I'm sorry about your name, Bubbles. Mum chose it, so I suppose you're stuck with it. I think you look like a Bob or a Thomas," Adam said, one day.

Mary stifled a giggle and Adam turned to her.

"Well, Bubbles isn't a proper name, is it? And he gets bored, Mum. I think he'd like a big arch to swim through. Matt's fish has got a brilliant one with tunnels and lights and everything."

Mary smiled. "And I suppose his fish is called Fred or John or something like that."

"Colin, actually."

"That figures. We'll buy Bubbles an arch – a small arch and I think that'll do for now."

Adam's loud snuffling brought Mary back to the present.

"Can we bury him, Mum? Like we did Grandad Ted and Daddy?" Adam said, pulling away from Mary and smearing snot all over his sleeve.

"Of course we can," Mary said, ashamed to find

herself thinking of a quick flush down the toilet. "I'll find a matchbox for him."

"A matchbox? Bubbles can't go in a matchbox. He... he..." Adam's face took on the pose of a screwed up ball of paper as more tears tumbled down his cheeks.

Mary bit her lip. Why did she always say the wrong thing?

"I know. Wait here," Adam said, brightening suddenly.

Mary stayed put, forcing her eyes away from the lifeless Bubbles, listening instead to the crash and bang of train sets, books, balls and cars being flung around Adam's room. She frowned. Adam wasn't usually one to get angry and take things out on his toys.

"It's all right, Mum, it's here somewhere," Adam shouted down the stairs.

Mary knew it was best not to ask. Nor to even think about it.

"Here it is. It's perfect," Adam said, jumping down the stairs two at a time.

Mary stared at the Action Man box, held lovingly in his arms.

"It's the scuba diving one. Bubbles will feel right at home in here."

Mary raised her eyebrows, knowing tears and tantrums would be forthcoming once Adam realised the box wasn't waterproof.

"I'm not going to put it in the tank, silly," Adam said and turned to Mary, one hand on hip.

Mary smiled at the younger version of herself.

"We'll bury him in the back garden like Grandad

Ted and Daddy were buried at the church. Can we have hymns, too? I'll put my Action Man in the box as well, and then he'll be just like Grandad Ted and Daddy. They aren't on their own either, are they?" Adam said, his lip starting to quiver once more.

"No, they're not on their own, Adam. They're up in heaven, aren't they, just like in the picture you drew. Do you remember?"

"Yeah, Grandad Ted was the striker, kicking a ball at Dad in goal."

"They were playing for their favourite teams, weren't they? They looked so happy because heaven's a very special place. Perhaps you could draw a new picture – one of Grandad Ted, Dad and Bubbles, all together in heaven."

"Fish don't play football, silly."

"How ridiculous of me to think so," Mary muttered.

She turned away and carefully scooped Bubbles from his watery home, laying him softly next to scuba diving Action Man, who was dressed for the part in wet suit, complete with the obligatory plastic knife. She almost felt sorry to be ending his life of adventure and reducing him to life in a box with a dead fish. Still, he was Action Man and she was sure he could cope.

Adam took the box and raised it over his head. He marched forward and the funeral procession began. Mary followed closely behind, her eyes fixed on the box as it wobbled and wavered from side to side.

"The door, Mum. Can you open the door?"

Mary leapt forward and opened the back door. Adam skilfully negotiated the step.

Mary jumped as her son launched into a dramatic version of, 'All Things Bright and Beautiful,' while making his way through the jungle of grass and weeds. Where on earth had he learned to sing like that? Mary's own voice was more karaoke than Kiri Te Kanawa and up to now, all Adam had seemed to do was scream and shout the lyrics of his favourite TV programmes.

"I'll stick him here, Mum. It'll be perfect. It's horrible and boggy here, so Bubbles will feel right at home. You'd better get a spade and dig him a hole, Mum. My hands are full," Adam, said, clutching the box tightly.

The tiny coffin fit snugly into its new grave.

"Goodbye, Bubbles, goodbye. Why did he have to die?" Adam said, taking her hand and his wails filled the air.

Mary shook her head, finding no answer. They stood there for a long time, staring at the Action Man coffin before placing the earth back on top and hiding it from view forever.

Mary read Adam a special story that night. It was one about heaven and how everyone in heaven was very happy because they could do their favourite thing.

"It's good in heaven, isn't it, Mum?" Adam said, kissing her goodnight.

"Yes, I rather think it is."

"Don't worry, Mum. I'll be all right. I loved Bubbles and I'll really miss him, but I've got you, haven't I? There's something for you downstairs. Something you need more than me," Adam said, squeezing her hand.

Mary closed his door quietly and tiptoed downstairs, with a frown on her face. As she entered the lounge, a picture on the coffee table caught her eye. It was a drawing. Dad was grinning in goal. Grandad Ted was smiling as he headed the football to Bubbles. Bubbles was in the middle under the most enormous archway, with lights flashing and tremendous tunnels going off to the side. He was leaping up and his tail was ready to flick the ball towards the net.

Mary started to cry. She clutched the picture to her chest. Adam was right. She did need it more than him. But she still had him – her Adam. She brushed her tears away and smiled.

The Shoplifter

Mary didn't want to go to jail.

"I didn't mean to do it. I'm not bad," she said, her pale blue eyes awash with tears.

She looked at the man. The shopkeeper. He looked at his wife. Well, Mary supposed it was his wife. They were wearing matching fluffy green jumpers with zig zags, spots and other jumbled patterns on them.

"I know that look, woman," the shopkeeper shouted, his bright beady eyes boring into his wife. "Don't you go feeling sorry for her. You always feel sorry for the shoplifters. Believe any old sob story, you would."

Mary watched his wagging finger, watched it weave its way from the wife to her, Mary.

"I know your sort. You're from that council estate. I bet you're a Griffiths. It's always a Griffiths."

"I'm not. My name's..." Mary stopped herself. Mary. Her name was Mary Bennett, but she couldn't tell them that. If they thought taking an apple was bad, then what on earth would they think when they found out about the terrible, terrible thing that she had done?

"That's it. Tell us your name, love. We can help

you," the shopkeeper's wife said.

"Shut up, Vi. She can tell us her name so we can call the police and they can sort her out."

"She must only be about seven," Vi said, folding her arms across a chest larger than any Mary had ever seen before.

Mary opened her mouth. She was eight and a quarter, actually. She closed her mouth. They didn't need to know that. They didn't need to know anything about her at all. She had never stolen anything in her life, but today she had slipped an apple into her pocket. But she was hungry, so very, very hungry.

"I don't care if she's a babe in arms," the shopkeeper's voice rose with each word.

"Roger, don't be so ridiculous."

Roger's finger was wagging wildly, jabbing itself into that enormous bosom and his face was flushing furious shades of purple. Neither of them seemed to notice Mary anymore. She knew the bell would give her escape away, but it would be too late by then – as long as they weren't fast runners and Mary was extremely certain they weren't.

It all went according to plan. In fact, better than any plan. Roger was the first to notice what was going on, though he chose to chase her with his mouth rather than making any movement after her.

Vi's voice carried to her as she hurried on, "Let her go. She hasn't even got the apple now. She left it behind."

Mary ran on and on until she was sure she could go no further. She looked at the streets and the lamps slowly coming to life. She looked into windows, seeing TV screens flickering and smelling dinners sizzling.

A mother hugged a daughter and ruffled her hair. Mary stopped. Her mum always ruffled her hair. She hated it. But right then, she would have given anything to have her mum ruffle her hair.

Mary wanted to cry, to feel great, gigantic tears tearing their way down her face. Her mum wouldn't ever ruffle her hair again. Mary had made sure of that.

She thought of her dad. He used to swing her up in his arms. Right from when she had been a baby. She loved her dad. And her mum. She had committed every feature, every smile, every line to memory. She'd had to do that because she wouldn't be seeing them ever again.

"Excuse me, love," a voice intruded upon her thoughts.

Mary swung round, feeling fear at the heavy breathing blasting into her ear.

"Sorry to startle you, love," Vi said, bending over and hugging her stomach, "blimey, that hurts. I haven't run in a long time."

Mary looked past the older woman, waiting for Roger to race round the corner.

"Don't worry about him, love. He's rigging up all sorts of traps and tests to stop shoplifters. Proper shoplifters. Not like you. Now, now then, don't cry. Tell Vi all about it," Vi said, stooping and putting her arms on the girl's shoulders. "Nothing can be that bad."

"But it is that bad," Mary sobbed.

"You look like you could do with a bite to eat. How about you come home with me and I'll make you something nice. Then you can tell me all about it."

Mary was transfixed by the hairy wart on Vi's chin. She forced her eyes away, then looked back again only to be confronted by its twin just under Vi's nose.

"Now, don't you worry about Roger. He's going to the bowls club straight from work. He wanted me to go with him, but it bores me to tears. What do you like doing, love?"

"I like ballet and gymnastics."

"How lovely. That's it, love. See, you've stopped crying now. Let's get home and have that bite to eat. Hey, I've got an idea. We pass the chippy on the way home. How about some fish and chips?"

Mary's stomach rumbled. Fish and chips were her favourite. Her mum and dad bought fish and chips as a special treat. The image of her mum and dad filled her head once more, bringing with them a fresh wave of tears.

"Here's a hanky, love. It's clean. Go on, wipe those eyes," Vi said and held out the floral cloth.

Mary took it and inhaled the sweet summery scent on its surface. She looked up at Vi. She looked like a mothball sort of lady, not a nice smelling one. Her Great Granny Edith was a mothball lady and Vi looked about her age. Mary looked at the warts once more. Great Granny Edith had at least ten warts, so perhaps Vi was a bit younger. Mary was also sure that Great Granny Edith wouldn't buy her fish and chips.

Vi held out her hand and Mary took it. They set off back the way they had come. Every now and then, Mary peeked out of the corner of her eye at her rescuer. Perhaps Vi would look after her now. Roger's rigid body and red face filled her mind. No, that wouldn't be any good, but perhaps Vi could look after her for a few hours anyway.

But what would happen after that? She couldn't go home. She couldn't go home ever again.

The salty smell wafted closer, announcing that they had almost arrived at the fish and chip shop. Mary looked at Vi's smiling face. Would Vi be buying her fish and chips if she knew the truth? Would she still be smiling if she knew Mary was a murderer?

By the time they reached Vi's house, every chip and every mouthful of fish was gone from Mary's portion, leaving only bones and paper soaked in vinegar behind.

"Goodness me, you were hungry," Vi said, turning the key in the door.

Mary followed her in, surprised by the neatness and order.

"Make yourself at home, love. How about a nice cup of tea?"

Mary screwed up her nose.

"Squash? Coke?"

Mary's eyes widened in delight. She wasn't allowed Coke at home.

"Coke it is then. I'm not too fond of the stuff myself, so if you don't mind, I'll put the kettle on. I'm gasping for a cup of tea."

Whilst the kettle made all sorts of spluttering noises, Mary let her eyes roam the room. There were photos everywhere. Black and white ones of a very slim Vi and a handsome-ish Roger on their wedding day. Colour ones of babies being bounced on knees and family photos with grandchildren. Despite Roger's rants back at the shop, she could tell they all loved one another. Each and every member of the family. Like her family had loved one another.

"There we are, love," Vi said, putting a huge glass of Coke in front of Mary.

Mary turned to her.

"I killed my parents," she said, then clapped her hands over her mouth.

Vi didn't hesitate for even a second. "Here's a choccy biccy to go with it. Now then, what's this about your parents?"

"I killed them."

"I'm sure you didn't, love."

"I did and they're going to send me to jail. I don't want to go to jail."

"You're not going to go to jail and you didn't kill your parents."

"I did. We were going to the zoo. It was my birthday. Two days ago. I wanted a computer, but they didn't get me one. We were in the car, almost there. I was being silly, saying horrible things. Mum turned round. She looked so cross. Dad turned to her and told her to leave it. Then we hit something. It was horrible. There was blood everywhere…a man came over…said they had to be dead. They weren't moving. Mum, nor Dad. I knew the man was right. They were dead. And I killed them."

"And so you ran."

"Yes, I ran," Mary said, her shoulders shaking as she gave in once more, "I didn't mean to. I love them."

Vi took Mary in her arms, letting the girl place her head on her shoulder until all her sobs were spent.

"You look like you could do with a bit of a rest. The spare bed's all made up," Vi said, "go up and have a little sleep. And don't go worrying about Roger. I can handle him. I've been handling him for far too many years than I care to think about."

Mary smiled. Sleep. That sounded good.

She didn't know how long she slept for. The knock downstairs jolted her awake instantly. Roger. Or the police. But Vi wouldn't have turned her in.

Voices came through the floorboards. High voices. Excited voices. They were coming upstairs. Thundering closer and closer. She held her breath, then punched it out.

The door burst open. Light blinded her. Hands reached for her. Perfume filled her nostrils. Expensive perfume. Familiar perfume.

"Mary, oh Mary," a deep voice. A croaky voice. A familiar voice.

"Mum! Dad!" Mary said, letting herself be caught up in their embrace. "You're not..."

"No, they're not, love. They're fine," a voice came from the doorway.

Mary looked up at Vi. The older woman winked.

"A few scratches and bruises, that's all," Mary's mum said, "but never mind, thank goodness this wonderful woman saw us on the news. It's all forgotten now."

"See, they're just fine," Vi said, "and so are you, love. So are you."

The Final Journey

I can't stand this. This is the worst journey of my entire life. I think I'm going to be sick. I wind the car window down and feel the short, sharp blast of early morning air. That's better. Stomach back under control. But I'm not. Now I'm going to cry.

I blink back the tears and look out the smeary window. A hint of blue tries its best to lighten the leaden-looking clouds. It doesn't succeed. Cows graze on grass, their mouths moving slowly, oblivious to the pricks of rain patting their skin.

I look away and find my eyes locking with a pair of brown eyes, eyes that I have seen far too much of over the past fortnight. Sandy, as she insisted I call her, reaches across and takes my hand.

"It's all right. Not long now," she says.

I pull my hand away. But what if it isn't all right? What if she's wrong? What if it's never all right ever again?

I think back to when I first met her – on that Monday afternoon two weeks ago.

"Hello, Mrs Martin, I'm Sandy," she said.

Sarah, Samantha, Sandy; it was all the same to me. I didn't care. I didn't care about anything at all. Only Kim. Kim was my world. Always had been, always would be, especially so since her dad, my husband, had died two years ago. We had clung to each other and helped each other get through. We were so close. I had thought nothing would ever come between us – until that Monday.

It had begun like any other week – frantically. Neither of us were morning people and that Monday we had overslept. The supervisor at the office had retired and the new one was intent on imposing her mark. Lateness was not something she tolerated. Things were going from bad to worse when Kim spilt her cornflakes and milk everywhere.

"Great! Another thing for me to clear up. Why can't you be more careful?" I had shouted.

Kim didn't say anything. She just slammed the door and stomped off to school. I never saw her again. Why did I shout at her? She could have covered the whole house in cornflakes and milk and it wouldn't have mattered. I could have been given the sack and that wouldn't have mattered either. Nothing mattered except my darling daughter.

I should have told her that I loved her, that she meant the world to me and that I never wanted to be without her whatever happened. But I didn't. I didn't say it.

The car stops. I look out the window. More cows. In the road this time. One stands right in front of the car. The driver hoots the horn. The cow continues to saunter across the road. Another one takes its place and decides to take a break from his journey. The horn is honked again and a fist shaken at the cow.

"It's really going to take notice of that, isn't it? What on earth did you do that for?" Sandy says, jabbing a long, bony finger into the driver's neck.

I remember saying almost the same thing to Sandy. It was the Wednesday by then. Forty-eight hours after Kim had gone missing.

"What on earth did she do that for? She never misses school and she certainly knows not to get into a stranger's car. It can't have been her," I had almost pleaded with Sandy.

But it was her. On the CCTV footage. 8.45 Monday 7th March when she should have been walking through the school gates. Instead she had been climbing into a battered old Ford Mondeo.

"Perhaps it wasn't a stranger. Perhaps she knew the driver," Sandy had suggested, every so politely.

I hated her then. Hated Sandy with her sleekly styled hair and carefully made-up face. I hated the soft, silky voice that I was sure every man loved. I hated her for her youth, her childless world. What did she know? What gave her the right to make assumptions about my daughter? I knew my daughter. Sandy didn't. She knew nothing about her.

I can feel Sandy looking at me as the car jolts into action once more leaving behind all the cows in their new grazing ground. I turn to her. See her smile. See her care. See beyond the pristine and perfect face she presents to the world.

I smile, too. She reaches out her hand and this time I squeeze it. Hold it. She feels my pain and I feel hers.

I think about the things she has told me, things many of her colleagues don't know. About her sister. The twin she thought she knew so well, but didn't know at all. Not until she was murdered by one of the clients she rented her body out to.

I couldn't hate Sandy then and yet I knew what she was implying. That I didn't know my own daughter. That perhaps we don't really know anyone. But I did know my daughter. Of course I did. Just because her sister had led a double life didn't mean my daughter did. My daughter wouldn't know anyone with a dented old car. She didn't like boys and certainly not boys old enough to drive. Yes, she had started to stay round her friends' houses and become more independent. She was nearly fifteen, beginning the gradual journey of leaving childhood and becoming a woman.

But she was still my little girl. I had felt her grow inside me and kick me with those tiny feet. I had given birth to her and nurtured her over the years. I knew everything about her.

But I didn't. Sandy was right. I didn't know about the boyfriend. The older man. Much older. I didn't know about the criminal record. GBH. Theft. Armed robbery. Sandy said his name was Ray. Friends gradually came forward and told the police how Kim had been seeing Ray for a few months. Ray's acquaintances were questioned. More of his sordid life was revealed.

The happy, fun-loving, carefree daughter I saw everyday wasn't the one everyone else knew. She had been. Oh yes, up until two years ago. I thought she had coped. I thought we had helped one another through the bad times.

She had coped with her father's death so much better than I. But she hadn't, not really. Things affect us all in different ways.

I am still looking at Sandy. She is staring ahead. I wonder if she is thinking about her journey. The final one to identify her sister's body. I shudder and feel the tears threaten again. She didn't tell me about it. She didn't want to go that far – for me or for her. But there was no one else. Mother, father and brother had all died in a car crash when she and her sister were in their late teens. How can I have thought she didn't understand? How could I have hated her?

Her head turns. She touches my shoulder. I wonder what made her tell me. What connected her to me. Maybe it was seeing the shock on my face when she told me about Ray. My face had crumpled. I know it had. Along with my whole world. She must have seen that same look plenty of times. On other mothers' faces. And yet she hadn't told them. Stay impartial, don't get too close. It's just a job.

Perhaps I reminded her of her sister. The sister she thought she knew. Sandy feels like a sister to me. A friend, too. A friend when no one else can find the right words to say. A friend who understands every heart-breaking moment you are going through and knows that every breath you take hurts each and every part of your body. A friend whose bond with you will never break. When something so bad, so appalling happens, how can something good emerge? Life does that.

I think about Kim when she was small. She loved her bedtime story. She always chose the stories about witches and monsters. No Cinderella or Prince Charming for her. She turned her nose up at fairytales. I laughed, so convinced she would meet her prince one day and I would watch her glide down the aisle in a flowing dress.

Maybe she will. I didn't think the phone call would ever come. She didn't speak at first. But I knew it was Kim. I couldn't speak either.

"Mum? Mum!"

"Kim!" I was shaking so much I could barely hold the receiver.

"I want to come home. I've made such a stupid mistake. I'm sorry, Mum, so sorry."

I had dreamt about hearing those words over and over. Deep down, I had thought a dream is all they would ever be.

Sandy's tearful eyes had mirrored my own and then she took over. Told me what to say, made phone calls and plans. Ray was apprehended. Kim taken to hospital. They said she was fine, but I wouldn't know that until I saw her. And I will see her in about five minutes. I can see the hospital in the distance.

What shall I do when I see her? Hug her? Tell her off?

The car has stopped now. I can see a sign for reception. I look at Sandy. My journey is ending so differently to hers. Did she think mine would be the same? Is that why she told me? She smiles, such a warm, happy smile. I know the answer.

I ask the way at reception and step into the lift. The doors close and I am carried upwards, the final stage of my journey. When the door opens, a new one will begin.

It won't be easy. There will be lots of tears and talking. Hard times, but hopefully plenty of good. At least I know where to start. I'll tell her I love her, that she means the world to me and I never want to be without her – whatever happens.

Going Home

I'm scared. I'm going home today. I'm not sure I want to. Mummy went all funny last time I was there. And I don't like it when she does that.

Grandad is packing cases into the car. I used to be a bit frightened of Grandad. He's got great big eyebrows that seem to dance every time he speaks and lots of lines on his forehead that jump into the middle of his face when he's cross. One of the giants in my book looks like him, but Grandad doesn't eat naughty boys like the giant does. And actually, Grandad's rather nice when you get to know him.

We didn't used to see very much of him or Granny before Mummy went funny. That's because they live miles and miles away, but I've been staying with them for a while now. It's been really good. They live by the sea, which isn't so good in winter though. I always thought it was sunny by the sea, but it's not been very sunny here.

Though, I have enjoyed walking along the beach with Grandad and Timmy, their Westie, as Grandad calls him. He looks like a fluffy bundle of white to me. A very nice bundle of white, not like any of the great big dogs my friends have. It was brilliant – just me, Grandad, Timmy and the waves. They were enormous waves crashing into the sand. And the wind. It's always windy here. I got to know Grandad on those walks. He would talk for ages about Mummy when she was small, about Uncle Trevor and Uncle Steve. And sitting in deck chairs and eating ice cream in the summer while the gulls squawked around him. About everything really.

Granny comes over and gives me a big hug. I think I am going to cry. I've always loved Granny. She is small with big glasses and a big smile. I like her hair. It's very curly and grey. Grandad said she used to dye it, but last time it went orange so she didn't dye it again. I wish she would. I would like to see her with orange hair. She's very good at cooking, too. Mummy isn't bad, but she doesn't make pies like Granny does.

"You are coming too, aren't you?" I ask her.

"Of course I am. You, me, Grandad and Timmy are all going to see Mummy. And we're going to stay for as long as you want us to," Granny says.

"For ever?"

Granny laughs. "Not for ever, Sam. For a while though. And then we have to come back here, to our house. But you can come and stay with us in the holidays if you like."

"All of the holidays?"

"We'll see," Granny laughs again.

Mummy always says that, too.

"Mummy is better now, isn't she?"

"Yes, much better," Granny says.

I look up into her grey eyes. They don't look so bright

anymore. I know what she is thinking. She is worried about the thing that made Mummy go funny – Daddy.

I think of him. He was tall. Very tall. I think I'm going to be tall, too. Just like Daddy. I hope so. He was handsome, too. I'm not sure I want to be handsome. Girls want to kiss you if you're handsome. Sally kissed me in the playground. It was horrible. The worst thing ever.

Daddy used to kiss Mummy a lot. Yuck. I'm never going to do that. He used to kiss me, too. On the top of the head. But that was all right.

"How do you feel about going home, Sam?" Granny interrupts me.

I look down at my boots. Daddy chose these. For when we played football together on a Sunday morning. Daddy used to be goalie. He was useless. I always scored at least ten goals.

"Sam?" Granny says.

"I'm okay about it. Do you think Mummy will go funny again?"

"I don't think so, Sam. We've talked to her on the phone lots and lots, haven't we?"

"Yes. She sounded okay. Not like last time I saw her."

"No, but we're going to look after her and make sure she's all right, aren't we?"

"Yes. I'm very good at looking after people. When Mummy had a very bad cold I took her breakfast in bed and I didn't spill a drop. I even did a bit of washing up, too."

"That's great, Sam," Granny says.

She is fiddling with the hem of her apron. She always

69

does that when she is worried about something.

"I'm all right about Daddy," I say.

"Oh?"

"We've talked about it, haven't we? I know Daddy's gone. He's up in heaven with God."

"Yes, he is, isn't he?"

"I think Daddy is very happy up there. He might even be a good goalie in heaven. Do you think God's good at football?"

"Yes, but not good enough to get a ball past your daddy," Granny says and hugs me again.

"Are you two ready then?" Grandad says, slamming the lid of the boot down.

Granny looks flustered and tugs her apron off. "Give me five minutes," she says.

Grandad's eyebrows start dancing. "Women," he mutters.

I giggle. Daddy always used to mutter that about Mummy, too.

I go and sit in the car. Daddy had a big Land Rover. It was great. I could see everything when I sat in that. Grandad's got a really little car, so I'm a bit squashed here in the back and I know that Timmy is going to leap all over me. At least we'll stop off lots. Grandad always needs the loo and they have burgers at the services.

Granny is ready now. She straps herself in.

"Got everything?" she says and turns to me.

"No! The picture – Mummy's picture," I say and ping the seatbelt off.

Grandad unlocks the front door for me and I hurry into the lounge. It is on the coffee table. I pick it up and look at it. I hope Mummy will like it.

I take it out to the car and get back in. Timmy is jumping all over me already. Now he is licking me. He's as bad as the girls.

Grandad revs the engine and we are on our way. I gulp. It will be strange without Daddy. Sometimes the house smelt of his work boots, especially on a Friday in summer. Mummy was always moaning at him to leave them in the garage. But he smelt nice when he put his aftershave on. He always put too much on, but Mummy liked it. I wonder what the house will smell like now.

"All right, lad?" Grandad says, catching my eye in the mirror just above his head.

I nod. Grandad looks back at the road. It isn't taking as long to get home as I thought it would. I wish it was.

We are stopping at the services. Grandad hurries inside, while Granny waits with me.

"Are you sure you're not hungry?" she asks.

I shake my head. I don't feel hungry at all.

"It'll be all right, Sam," Granny says.

She leans over in her seat and takes my hand. I pull it away. I'm going to cry and I don't want to cry.

Granny gets out the car and squeezes in the back with me. She cuddles me. It feels nice, but I can't stop crying.

"Let it out. Let it out," she says and strokes my back.

We stay like that for a long time and then Grandad is back. He doesn't say anything, just waits for Granny to get back into the front. Then he winks at me in the mirror. I wink back. He smiles and looks proud. I couldn't wink before I came to stay with Grandad. I smile, too and then he turns and gives me a packet of chewy fangs. They're my favourite.

"Thanks, Grandad," I say and offer them round.

Granny and Grandad shake their heads. They don't know what they're missing.

I can't believe we are almost home. I wonder if it will look different. We turn the corner. Our house is number 21 on the left. It looks just the same, but Daddy's Land Rover has gone. Grandad said it was a bit poorly after the crash. Mummy's car is in the drive.

I look up at the house and at the kitchen window. Daddy isn't there. He always waited for me there.

Mummy opens the door and is walking towards us. I look at her face. She looks so sad. She sees me and she is smiling. She is running now. I am out the car and running, too. She scoops me up in her arms and swings me round.

"Cor, you've grown. What has that Granny been feeding you?" she says and puts me to the ground.

I laugh and give her the picture. Her smile goes as she looks at it. I hope she isn't going funny again. Now she is going to cry. I thought she would like it. It's of me and Mummy in the garden. We are playing and smiling as we look up at Daddy high in the sky in heaven. He is smiling, too.

"It's beautiful, Sam," she says and smiles again, 'and so are you. It's good to have you home.'

She hugs me and I hug her as tight as I can.

The Right Thing

She could do it. There. She'd taken one step. Now two. Carrie turned and looked behind her. Sasha was still there, one fist pounding into the other one. Carrie gulped. She shouldn't have looked.

She turned back. Took another step and stopped. She couldn't go on. She couldn't do it. She closed her eyes. Felt a tear fall.

"Hurry up, Baxter. I haven't got all day," Sasha's guttural voice said.

A shiver swept through Carrie's body. She pushed it away and thought of her mum at home instead – thought of that warm smile, the softness of skin as her mum stroked her hand and the gentle voice, which always said everything would be ok.

But it wasn't ok. Perhaps if her mum were there, right now, then everything would be ok. And her dad. She smiled, thinking of her dad and that rapidly greying hair. Poor Dad. It was no wonder after everything he'd been through.

"Baxter! Now!" that vile voice again.

No, it was just as well that they weren't there. They

would hate to see her like this.

She walked on, slow at first, then gaining momentum. Perhaps it wouldn't be so bad after all. If she just did it, then it would all be over. She felt the lump in her throat growing larger and larger. It wouldn't be over. It would just be the start.

Her eyes flitted sideways, glimpsing the building, small, yet a giant's den at that precise moment in time. She looked down at her feet.

"Go on, Baxter. Get in there. Now! You've got five minutes. That's your limit. Best way's straight in, grab it and straight out. Got it?"

Carrie's head snapped up and she stared at the shop. 'Freedlands' News' was lit up in brilliant blue lettering.

She knew the Freedlands. So did her mum and dad.

"Hard workers. They nearly lost everything a few years back and what with all these supermarkets taking the lion's share of the market, it's a wonder they're able to keep going at all," Carrie had heard her dad say to Mum a while ago.

What would they say if they knew what she was about to do?

"Four minutes," the voice was fainter now, but the meaning behind the words no less fierce.

Carrie thought about running away in the opposite direction. If she went up the lane, it would get her back home and away from Sasha. But Sasha would know exactly where she was going. She'd probably double back and be waiting for her when Carrie reached the end of the lane.

Even if she outran Sasha, what good would it do her?

Everyone knew about Sasha Wickens. She was in Year 10. Carrie was in Year 9. Sasha always picked on the younger and quieter ones. She was usually surrounded by her four followers, all from Year 10. When Carrie had said she would nip round the shop for her mum and Sasha had jumped out, Carrie braced herself, waiting for the others to leap out, too. When they hadn't, Carrie didn't feel any easier, especially when Sasha had looked her straight in the eye.

Carrie knew she had been lucky to escape Sasha so far. She'd known it was only a matter of time before Sasha turned her attention to Carrie. When Carrie had caught sight of Sasha while she was out with her mum and dad the weekend before and seen the smirk slowly spread on the older girl's face, she knew that time had come.

"Three minutes."

Carrie had to do it. It wasn't just about her. Others would suffer too. Her mum. Her dad.

She pushed the door. Heard the bell tinkle.

"Hello, Carrie. How are your mum and dad?" Mrs Freedlands said, smiling widely at her.

"Fine," Carrie said, her voice sounding shaky even to own ears. "Thank you."

"Is everything all right, love?" Mrs Freedlands asked.

Carrie looked on, beyond Mrs Freedlands, at the TV showing the movements of everyone in the shop. Carrie was amazed that Sasha hadn't been caught before now. Perhaps she had been or more likely, she made others do her dirty work for her.

"Carrie?"

"Yes, I'm fine thank you, Mrs Freedlands. I've not

been well…had a bit of a cold…um, that's all," Carrie said.

Now Sasha had her lying. Carrie quickly moved along to the toiletries aisle. Sasha wanted a can of 'Sergeant's Super Slick Hairspray.' Carrie tugged her fingers through her own hair. She'd never thought about using hairspray. Her mum used 'Elnett.' Carrie sniffed, almost able to smell its sweet scent. She hugged her stomach, swinging slightly from side to side.

There had to be only two minutes left now. Her eyes roamed the shelves, searching for the can. Up and up they went. Her eyes stopped. There it was. Huge. Looming right at the back of the top shelf.

What would happen if she didn't walk out with it? Her mum. Her dad. Sasha had already made the threats.

"I saw your mum last week. What happened to her legs? Did you make a joke and she laughed so hard they fell off? And your dad? Did someone poke him in the eyes? There are names for people like that. And I'm not frightened to tell them," Sasha had said only a moment ago, though it felt more like a lifetime ago.

Would Sasha really carry out her threat? Would she hurt those two, wonderful, caring people more than they had already been hurt?

"I'll do it and all. Then I'll run off with your mum's wheelchair and your dad won't be able to do anything about it because he can't see a thing," Sasha had continued, laughing at her own words.

No. Carrie couldn't let that happen. Not after everything. She closed her eyes, thinking back to the day of the accident. It had been the third week of the summer holidays. She was staying at her best-friend's parents' house for a few days while Mum and Dad went to look after Grandma, who had been diagnosed with diabetes. She could remember when the call came through so clearly, but not as clearly as when she had first seen them lying there in their hospital beds.

They both blamed themselves. Dad for driving badly. Mum for nodding off and not noticing the van careering across the motorway. But it was the van driver's fault. It all came out at the inquest. He was three times over the alcohol limit. It didn't matter. The damage was done.

It wasn't easy, but they coped. Little by little. Slowly, the smiles came back and the yearn for life and living. They said they couldn't have done it without Carrie. They needed her. They loved her. They wouldn't want her to do this.

Carrie was certain there couldn't even be a minute left now. But she wasn't going to take the hairspray. She was going to turn and walk right out that door. And then what? Run away? No, she was going to confront Sasha. She was going to tell her that she hadn't got her precious hairspray. Sasha wouldn't really do it. Even she couldn't be that callous. Surely? Maybe she would come after Carrie instead. But what could one girl do to her that was that bad? She would probably fetch her friends and then they would hurt her, really hurt her.

But not like her mum and dad. No, seeing her parents go through that pain, that suffering and that perseverance was worse than anything they could do to her.

The tinkle of the bell stopped all thought. Her time was up. She edged towards the end of the aisle and peered round.

"Has my magazine come in yet?" an old lady was asking Mrs Freedlands.

Carrie let out a big sigh, then sucked it up again. Now it was her time. Time to face Sasha.

But first, Carrie was going to make her wait. She had come on an errand for her mum and she was going to complete that errand. She took the crumpled list from her pocket and didn't stop until she had everything.

Several minutes later, she left the shop with the tinkle of the bell ringing in her ears. She let the door slowly pull to behind her and stood very still on the step. She couldn't see Sasha, but already she felt her presence. She swallowed. It was all very well, thinking about facing her, being brave and making a stand. It was a very different matter to do it.

"Psst. I said five minutes. That was ten. You're done for," Sasha said.

Carrie walked forward, trembling with each step she took towards the corner.

"You've got a bag. You bought the stuff! I'm going to do what I said, you loser," Sasha said, roaring round the corner out of her hiding place and reaching for the bag.

"No, you're not," Carrie said, pulling the bag back and out of Sasha's reach.

"What?"

"You're not going to do anything, because you'll just be wasting your time.

You can't hurt my family any more than we've already been hurt," Carrie said, feeling a strength she didn't know she had.

"Oh."

"Now, why don't you go and do something nice for a change?" Carrie continued.

"What?"

"You don't know how to, do you? Just remember one thing. One day, you'll get your comeuppance. Bullies always do," Carrie said.

She looked at Sasha. The other girl opened her mouth, but nothing came out. Carrie walked by her towards home – home to her mum and dad. She didn't know what would come of that afternoon's events, or if she had done the right thing, but somehow, she thought she had.

The Intruder

"Oh dear, oh dear, oh dear," Tom muttered, staring at his home of the past forty years.

It wasn't much of a home really, more of a hut, but it was his home. And someone was in it.

He shook his head. He had only been gone twenty minutes. He quite fancied some rabbit for his tea, so he had taken a stroll into the woods. He had never been very good at catching things, except coughs and colds, so there he was empty handed and with an intruder in his home.

He took a step forward, cursing as his boots squelched in a muddy puddle. He felt the murky liquid ooze onto his holey socks and snake up between his toes. He grimaced and pushed on, pounding towards home.

He stopped outside, his head thumping and a sickness forcing its way into his throat. Hardly a soul had bothered him in all his years there. He grunted as if a fist had flailed him in the stomach. Someone had to own the hut. He was surprised he hadn't been thrown out years before. Where would he go?

He closed his eyes and raw and ragged memories

surged into his mind. He had known life on the streets. He wouldn't want it again.

A wail from within the hut pricked at his chest, punching the air from his lungs. Perhaps it was an injured animal, but he was sure there had been a face at the window.

Tom pushed the door and watched as the jagged oak panels effortlessly swung back. This time there was a definite cry – a human cry and one of fear. Feet flew over the stone floor scrambling for safety.

"It's all right. It's only old Tom. I won't hurt you," Tom's gruff voice wasn't the most melodious.

The room wasn't very big and the furniture was sparse, shielding no one. Tom's eyes fell on the young girl huddled by the rickety cupboard in the corner.

"Please, lass, don't be frightened," Tom reached out his hand.

The girl gasped as if touched by a ferocious spark of fire. She pulled back, moulding herself to the wall.

Tom took a step back. The last time he had caught sight of his own reflection, he had scared himself, so it was no wonder the girl was petrified. When he was a lad he was lucky if he had a bath once a week. Time had only worsened matters and his home boasted no comforts like a bath. He knew his beard needed a trim and if he didn't detangle it soon, he would have birds setting up home in it. His clothes weren't the best either, not that he had ever been one for fashion, but he had seen better on a scarecrow.

Tom walked over to the table taking centre stage. He brushed crumbs and wodges of month-old food from the wood and sat down. He didn't often care about his attire or what others thought of him, but suddenly it mattered.

A smile slowly spread over his face and beneath the grime, the handsomeness that could have been revealed itself. He pushed himself up and fetched a box from the side. He took out a bun brimming with icing. Rabbit followed by a bun would have made a smashing dinner, but he had no rabbit and now it looked like he would have no bun. His mouth watered and he wished the lady at the park had thrown the other one in the bin as well. But from the way her lips smacked, smearing the icing all round her plump face, he had been fortunate she hadn't scoffed them both.

He held the bun in front of him and trod like a child trying not to spill his drink. He set the bun down on the table and walked towards the door. There he paused and forced himself not to look at the girl, before stepping outside.

Tom stood and witnessed the cool autumn sun begin its descent and the wind whip round his ankles, a warning of the winter to come.

He listened to the scurry of feet and the chair scraping back. Should he wait? He listened. Silence. He opened the door. The girl couldn't have been any more than fifteen. Chocolate brown eyes gazed up at him from behind an overgrown fringe of mousy hair.

"Go on, that's it. Enjoy the cake," Tom said, moving forward with each word. "You're a run away, aren't you, lass?"

The girl looked ready for flight.

"No, lass, don't go. I understand. You see I'm a run away, too."

The brown eyes searched his face and she frowned, but her shoulders relaxed a little. Tom pulled out the other chair and looked to the girl for approval. She nodded, though still wary of her host.

Tom sighed and as words tumbled from his mouth, the years fell away. He was ten years old again. The war had ended. England was victorious and people were dancing in the streets. But not Tom.

His Aunt Ethel stood in front of him and a shroud of darkness hung over her from head to toe. His father always said his mother's sister was a witch. It was their secret. His father would tuck him into bed every night and they would tell each other stories about Aunt Ethel and her broomstick. But Tom hadn't wanted to laugh anymore. Not now his mother and father were dead, taken away by the cruelness of war. Not now he would be moving to Scotland for a new life with Aunt Ethel.

Tom had soon found out she wasn't a witch. He wished she had been. After the passing of sixty years, the physical scars had vanished, but the mental ones would always remain.

Tom's mind and body could bear no more and he had run until he could run no longer. Street-life had not come easy to the young lad, but he had turned his hand to anything and he soon began to make a life for himself. The years passed and with them the shedding of childhood and the emergence of a man. Lucy had come along and Tom felt happiness beckon.

As Tom retold his tale, tears came to his eyes as he remembered John, the loan shark. Tom never forgave himself for borrowing the money in the first place and when they took his Lucy, his life was over.

"You ran again, didn't you?" the young girl interrupted his reminiscence.

"I did indeed, lass. I went running for years until I found this place and here I've stayed. What for, I don't know. I don't know," Tom whispered, his body shaking with sobs.

A hand covered his. Tom almost recoiled from the contact. It was so long since he had felt another's touch. He looked up at the girl and felt her warmth spread throughout him. Her eyes glistened with tears.

"So what's made you run away, lass?" Tom snorted, drying his eyes with an old rag.

"Nothing like what you've been through," the girl started sheepishly.

"Come now, something's made you run."

She nodded and patted her stomach. Tom's eyes followed, taking in the expanding waistline.

"Your lad left you as well, eh?"

Again, the nod.

"I failed my exams, too," she said, giving in to a further flurry of tears.

"You're in a bit of a pickle there, but it's not all bad. I bet your mum and dad are worried about you. Expect they'd give anything to have you back home. What's your name, lass?"

"Bethany. As mums and dads go, they're great, but they'll kill me for this," she couldn't go on.

"I doubt that. I doubt that very much. Of course they'll be mad at first, but you're their daughter. They'll help you through it all, every step of the way, lass. You've got to go back to them. Don't end up like me."

Bethany squeezed Tom's hand. Neither needed to speak.

Darkness had descended and caught them unawares. Tom walked over to the ancient gas fire. One day he knew it wouldn't turn, but it had been one of his most faithful friends. He made a sumptuous supper of beans on toast and the two talked until the early hours of the morning like age-old friends.

Sunlight stabbed his eyes and Tom roused himself from a peaceful sleep. He hoped Bethany didn't mind beans on toast again. Perhaps he would push the boat out and go and get some eggs. Old Farmer Joe was good to him.

Tom glanced round the room. He was alone. He pushed himself to his feet and found the note on the table.

Dear Tom,
I rang Mum on my mobile. She cried and asked me to come home. She said she loved me and she would be there for me whatever I've done.
Thank you, Tom. I'll always remember you. You are an angel sent from heaven.
Lots of love,
Bethany

"Drat," Tom said, knowing he was going to cry and trying to find his rag. Though, for some reason, he couldn't help, but smile. Maybe it was because he had his home back to himself again, but he rather thought it was for another reason.

Waiting

George was going to die. His weather-beaten face was going through the whole spectrum of Teletubbies: yellow, green, red and finally purple. His bushy brows furrowed then did a little pirouette to see how high they could go. His lips quivered, twitching before his false teeth clamped down on them. This was awful. He couldn't take much more.

It was late September, but for some reason the string vest and best beige shorts felt like a fur coat. He clutched his chest, feeling its beat building to a crescendo like a volcano waiting to spill piping hot lava onto the unsuspecting hoards below.

He thought of Sheila. He had to fight it. He couldn't let her see him like this. He took a deep breath, gagging as a fly looped the loop into his mouth.

Specks of spittle gathered at the side of his lips as the fly's wings tickled his tongue. As George opened wide and the fly spluttered to the floor, he heard the kitchen door open. It was Sheila. She'd come.

George wiped his eyes. It wasn't supposed to be like this. The day had started so well, but this was the moment he had been waiting for. But what if Sheila ruined it? And she could so easily. Perhaps she didn't care anymore. Maybe she no longer loved him.

George stared at his sandals. They were lovely sandals, though the white socks probably didn't show them off to their best. Neither did the earwig staggering across them. George thought about flicking it off. He couldn't move. If he moved he would have to face Sheila.

He could feel her eyes boring into him. At least she had come. That had to mean something, surely?

His nostrils took on a life of their own. He could smell something. It was probably nothing. His hearing aid screeched in his ear. People were gathering, crowding round him. Voices chanting, breaths on his face.

His eyes blurred, a mist of tears hanging over them. This was it. He dared to look.

The crowd parted and Sheila stood before him. Her beautiful face lit up the room as she walked towards him. There was something in her hands. Could it be?

It wasn't. The choke caught in his throat and he fought for breath. His head pounded and the room was spinning.

"Come on, let's get you sat down," Sheila said, smoothing everything over as always, "look what I've got. It's come."

He shoved the envelope aside. "Don't want it."

"All right, all right. I remembered. You and your chocolate cake," Sheila said, fetching the huge mountain of sponge from the kitchen.

George felt the tears roll down his cheeks, though this time they were for a different reason.

"To the Best Dad in the World. Happy 100th," he read the words on the cake.

Shouts and clapping filled the room. George looked at the envelope. He supposed he had better see what the Queen had to say.

In and Out

"You can't retire. You're only seven," Susan said.

"Grandad is retiring, so I'm retiring, too," George said and folded his arms tightly across his chest.

Susan looked at the set of the jaw, the stern, blue eyes and ears flushing flaming pink in anger. Susan sighed. He was more like his grandfather than he would ever know.

"So what has your grandad told you about retirement then?" Susan said.

"He said it's when you've been doing something for a long, long time and you're fed up with it so you retire and you don't ever have to do it again," George said, proudly.

"What wise words. Thanks, Dad," Susan muttered, before raising her voice, "well, your grandad has been working for the bank for forty-five-years, which is a long, long time."

"I know. I can count way past forty-five, Mum."

"Well," Susan resumed, doing her best impersonation of a cool, calm and very collected mother, "your grandfather is sixty-three, which is quite old."

"I can count way past sixty-three."

"I know," Susan said, her teeth, her fists, in fact everything clenching and she abandoned all pretence of cool, calm and even the slightest bit collected. "Your grandfather is retiring from the bank after years and years of working. You haven't even started work yet, so how on earth can you retire?"

George looked up at his mum. He shook his head. "You just don't understand. I've been a child for a very long time and to be quite honest with you, I'm fed up with it. I think it's time for me to retire," George said, sticking his nose up in the air.

A noise escaped from Susan's lips. It was immediately followed by another. Then she could bear it no more. Laughter burst forth and she hugged her sides. A seven-year-old fed up with being waited on hand and foot, fed up with playing games all weekend and having to put up with four times as much holiday per year than Mr. Davenport at the office had written into her contract. The sheer torture!

George glared at his mother. He stomped past her and upstairs to his room.

*

George sat down on his bed. It was all right for her. She was a grown-up. Grown-ups knew everything. Grown-ups could do what they wanted. Well, he would show her. He wasn't a child anymore. He had retired. He was a grown-up now, too. Connor at school said people retired when they were sixty-five and his grandad wasn't sixty-five yet. And Connor was always right. Connor knew everything about everyone and everything there was to know in the whole wide world. So if grandad could retire early, then so could he.

George grinned. A grown-up. He was a real live grown-up. His dad would be so proud of him. Now he was a grown-up he could drive to see his dad. Driving was so easy. He had done it on the dodgems at the fair last week. He had no idea why you weren't allowed to drive until you were seventeen. That was years and years away. Still, it didn't matter now. He was a grown-up.

The only difficulty was which sort of car he would choose. A Porsche? No, his dad said Ferraris were better. George could just see his dad's face when he pulled up outside his house in a racing red Ferrari.

But if he went to his dad's house he would have to see Dawn, too. What a stupid name that was. And he would have to see the new baby. They had called her Skye. That was even worse than Dawn. George supposed her eyes were blue like the sky on a sunny day, but the sky was grey more than blue where they lived. He laughed. Perhaps they should have called her Raincloud instead.

Maybe he could take his dad out to lunch instead. Then he wouldn't have to see Raincloud. His dad sometimes took him to McDonald's and there was a McDonald's just down the road from his dad's house. George noticed these things. George suddenly had a terrible thought. He wouldn't be able to have a kids' meal anymore and most importantly of all, that meant no toy. And he was sure it was rockets this week. Ones that made great loud noises and flashed on and off.

He pushed the idea of toys from his mind. He was a grown-up. He didn't need toys anymore. Perhaps they ought to go to a café or something, somewhere where they had posh food. George screwed up his nose. That meant vegetables. But grown-ups loved vegetables, didn't they?

Thoughts of vegetables were soon replaced by a very wonderful thought indeed. Grown-ups didn't go to school. No more wearing silly shorts in the summer, no stinky, squeaky plimsolls in P.E. or stupid spelling tests. No getting up early for a wash or not being allowed to stay up.

He could watch grown-up telly, too. He chewed on his lip, twisting it one way, then the other. Did grown-ups watch Power Rangers? They watched Star Wars and that was cool, so that would be all right. His mum liked soppy films, though. Ones where people kissed and said they loved each other. George thought he would steer clear of those. Things blowing up, car chases and sword fights. That sounded more like it.

Grown-ups swore, too. His mum did, especially when she was talking about his dad. George swore, too. Though he hoped his mum never found out. He used the b-word a lot at school. Bum. He giggled. He was a grown-up now, so it didn't matter if she did find out.

He gasped. She said if she ever heard him swear she would stop his pocket money. But grown-ups didn't get pocket money. They got proper money. Pounds and pounds of it. Not a stingy £5 a month.

Grown-ups had to earn their money and work very hard. His mum was always telling him that. George was going to earn his own money, too, but going to work couldn't be that hard. Not as hard as school work anyway.

Now he was a grown-up he could be a fireman and leap down the pole and into the brilliant red fire engine and save people's lives. Or he could be a policeman and chase criminals round the streets. A spaceman sounded even better. Especially being able to use a light-sabre. George already had one of those and he had been practicing. Even if he said so himself, he was pretty good. He could beat Connor and no one ever beat Connor at anything.

A huge poster on his bedroom wall caught his eye. Frank Lampard, from the best football team in the world stared down at him. George was going to play for Chelsea, too. He would score lots and lots of goals and earn lots and lots of money. His mum always said footballers earned far too much so he was definitely going to be a football player.

Though, if he was a grown-up, he would have to take his posters down. Grown-ups had pictures of fields full of sheep on their walls. His mum had one of a house stuck on the side of a mountain in her bedroom. George thought Frank looked a lot better on the wall.

George's stomach was rumbling. He looked at his watch. Lunchtime. He grinned. His mum had promised him Spiderman pasta shapes for lunch. But he couldn't have silly shapes if he was a grown-up. He would have to have Linguini instead. Whatever that was, but it was something his mum talked about. He supposed he wouldn't be able to have his Teenage Mutant Ninja Turtles cup and plate anymore either.

Instead of Ribena, he would have to drink coffee, which looked the colour of a cow-pat. Maybe that was just how his mum made it. Connor liked coffee. Perhaps Connor's mum made nice coffee.

George suddenly remembered something very important. His grandad was taking him to the park the next day. Grown-ups didn't run up slides or swing on monkey bars. But George liked the park.

George jumped as the doorbell rang. Connor! Connor was coming for lunch and to play Power Rangers. But George wouldn't be able to play Power Rangers if he was a grown-up. His dad tried to play it with him sometimes, but he wasn't very good. He looked more like a gangly gibbon than a fabulous fighter. Grown-ups were useless at playing. George sighed. He didn't want to be useless at playing, too.

George thought about his grandad. There was something else grandad had said about retirement, something that he hadn't told his mum. Grandad had said he might not like retirement and if he didn't, he could come out of retirement and go back to work. George didn't think he liked being a grown-up. As Connor burst through George's bedroom door, George grinned.

It was time to come out of retirement and go back to being a child.

A Special Friend

I didn't know what had happened. Not at first. And then I knew. I didn't hurt anymore.

It was wonderful. I had always hurt. I couldn't remember a time when I didn't hurt. But there must have been a time. Once. Before the beatings began. Before Mummy and Daddy died.

I can't remember my mummy and daddy. They look nice in the photographs, but everybody looks nice in photographs. Even Aunt Maud and Uncle Frank look nice in photographs. They look very old. As Aunt Maud kept telling me, Mummy was a mistake. Granny Violet had wanted to 'get rid of her' because she didn't want to have any more children, but the doctors said she was too late. I'm glad she was too late.

I don't mind old people. Father Christmas is old. He didn't ever come to Aunt Maud and Uncle Frank's house, but he came to school once. I wanted to go with him when he left. I thought I could go and help him with the reindeers. I told Father Christmas I could help to make all the toys, too and fly with him round the world on Christmas Eve. He laughed and ruffled my hair. How

I wished I could have gone with him.

Aunt Maud and Uncle Frank were nice at first. They didn't have children of their own. They hadn't been 'blessed' with them, they said. They told me I was a 'gift from God,' that He had taken away my parents so that their lives were complete.

And then they changed. It was Aunt Maud at first. I was getting ready for school one morning and my nail went through my tights. I laughed and went to get another pair. There weren't any in the drawer. When I asked Aunt Maud if she had anymore, she struck me to the ground. It hurt. How it hurt. I remember turning to her and looking up at her, waiting for her to say she was sorry, that she didn't know what had come over her.

Perhaps she would hug me to her and kiss my head. She didn't. She stood there, with her hand on her hip and her foot tapping. Her face was red and her lips white where her teeth were chomping down on them. My eyes went up to her nose and the nostrils, narrow one minute and wide the next. Up my eyes went to hers, usually so clear and blue, but cloudy and cold then. I had seen books with pictures of werewolves, vampires and all sorts of creatures on them. I had thought they were stories. I wasn't so sure anymore.

Aunt Maud opened her mouth then, that very wide mouth, hidden most of the time by thin, chapped lips. I was certain she was going to eat me whole.

"You evil child. The Bible tells of children born of the devil, Lucy. I always detested your mother. Right from the moment she was born. I rejoiced when she died. And that no-hoper father of yours. Then I thought we had been given a chance to put right a wrong. But you're just like them. You must be punished. The Bible insists upon it," I was sure the words flew from her mouth.

They were words I never forgot. They weren't the last either.

Uncle Frank wasn't so bad, but Aunt Maud lied. She told him about things I hadn't done. She told him I was wicked and that I did terrible things to her. He believed her. Then he would come to me and beat me. He was so big, so strong, so powerful. Afterwards, he told me not to cry and said that he was sorry. He hugged me and his own tears joined mine. As quickly as they had come, those tears dried when Aunt Maud came to inspect his work.

School was the only place where I could get away. I loved school. The teachers talked about what wonderful things I could do when I grew up. Policemen and nurses came to school to talk about their jobs. The teachers told me I could be anything I wanted to be as long as I worked hard. I learnt about foreign countries and lands far, far away. I made friends, too.

I thought Aunt Maud would be pleased. I thought she would want me to do well, to be good and to be liked by the teachers and children. She didn't and she tried to take me away from school. She said I had to stay home with her. She made me cook and clean. She told me she would teach me all I needed to know. She said I had been getting above my station, that I was too stupid to learn and to make something of myself. She told me I wouldn't ever go to school again.

But she couldn't do that. The school kept ringing and then they came round. I thought about telling them everything. Maybe they would take me away and I could go and live with someone nice who didn't hurt me.

Aunt Maud was so nice to them. She made them lots of tea and brought them her best biscuits. They liked Aunt Maud. They believed every word she said.

At least it meant I could go back to school. There was nothing Aunt Maud could do. It was the law.

"But don't go getting any grand ideas. You're nothing. You're worthless. And I don't want to hear about any friends, either. I've put the school right about you, young lady. I told them what a wicked child you are and how they don't see what you're really like."

Her words worked. Everyone was different towards me when I went back to school. All I wanted was a friend. Just one special friend. But I had no one.

*

I had often thought about ghosts. I'm sure every child thinks about ghosts. I wasn't sure I believed in them, but when you become one, you have to. It was a bit strange, seeing my body, so small, so stiff, there in Uncle Frank's arms.

"What have you done? What have you done, woman?" he shouted at Aunt Maud.

It all went a bit mad then. Uncle Frank lost it. Aunt Maud went purple before Uncle Frank let go of her neck. I was glad he did. She wouldn't have made a very nice ghost.

Then the sirens started. People came running in. Policemen. Ambulance men. Voices shouted. People prodded and poked at my body. Aunt Maud was quiet, so very quiet. Her body was still, like one of the stuffed teddies I had until Aunt Maud threw them out. Uncle Frank just sobbed, shaking with hulking great tears.

"Why? Why didn't I stop her? I knew. I knew what she was doing. I knew she'd go too far one day. I failed you, Lucy," he said, over and over and then he ran to my body and lay protectively across it.

I think Uncle Frank will make a nice ghost one day.

I didn't know what to do then. I didn't want to stay there anymore. But I didn't know where to go. I felt something tug me. I wondered if I was going up to heaven. All little girls and boys went up to heaven, apart from me. I wasn't nice. I wasn't as bad as Aunt Maud said I was. I was certain of that, but I had to be a little bit bad, otherwise she wouldn't have hurt me.

I wasn't tugged upwards, so I knew I wasn't going to heaven. I wasn't tugged down either, so I wasn't going to that other horrible place. Instead, I was tugged sideways, right through the wall and out, away from Aunt Maud and Uncle Frank. I was pulled further, across hills and hedges, fields and forests. I didn't want to stop. I felt free, flying away from everything.

And then the tugging stopped. Just like that. I didn't see him to start with. He was only little. Like me. He was crying. He looked so lost, so sad just sat there on a small stonewall outside a little house. I wanted to hug him and to tell him everything would be all right.

But I couldn't. I would have frightened him if I had done that. My arm would probably have gone right through him and then he would really have started to cry. And scream. People would have come running and

I'd probably have been reported to the Ghost Council or whatever it was called. They might have made me go back to Aunt Maud.

Something shiny caught my eye. It was a ball. A bright, blue ball. I pushed it along the ground towards the boy and turned away. I had to go. I couldn't help him. Then I looked back. I don't know why I did. The boy was looking straight at me.

I waited for the scream. It didn't come. Instead, he pushed the ball back to me, his tears slowing.

"Can you see me?" I asked.

"You're a ghost. Of course I can see you," he said.

"How do you know?"

"Because I'm a ghost, too. I don't want to be a ghost," he said and started to cry harder.

I did hug him then. And he hugged me back. It felt so good to be hugged. He couldn't stop crying and then I found that neither could I. We didn't stop crying for ages.

His name's Sam. He had a lovely mummy and daddy. A brother and sister, too. He didn't want to die, but the Leukaemia took over. We've taken it one day at a time, little by little and Sam doesn't cry so much now.

When I first saw him, I wondered if I had been sent to help others. Now I know I have. There's a little girl who's been in an accident and who looks very unsure. Sam was my first friend. My first special friend. Now I know there's going to be many more.

Sam

—

Why did she do it? Why did she come through the park? She could have gone the long way round. They wouldn't have gotten to her then.

Tom looked at his watch. Any moment now, the school gates would swing open to release hundreds of children. Plenty of them came through the park, especially on a Friday. Great, big grins were plastered on faces, bags were whizzed round in the air and shirt collars loosened.

Tom smiled, hearing the chatter and excitement as the first ones raced along the path. It was always the youngest ones who came first, having been let out that little bit earlier. Mums weren't far behind, pushing buggies overflowing with bags and books, little ones gripping their hands while the mums caught up on all the latest news. They made for the playground and it was soon full of bouncing babies and boys bellowing as they leapt onto roundabouts and raced round. Tom watched a little girl climb anxiously up the tallest slide and then he smiled at the glee spreading across her face as she hurtled down to the bottom.

That was what made his job worthwhile. He could

cope with anything then. Even the fact that his own children and grandchildren were so far away. One daughter had been dazzled by the beauty of New Zealand and taken up residence there, while the other was closer, in France, though sometimes it may as well have been the other side of the world. Still, they were all coming over for Tom's big one at Christmas. Sixty. He couldn't believe it. He could remember when both daughters had been born and then when he'd taken the job at the park. Grandchildren had come in the blink of an eye. Where did all that time go?

And then he saw her. Sam. She didn't look like one of the older ones. She was so small and with those big, brown eyes so wide, she seemed smaller still. Tom wondered where her mother was. If only her mother walked with her, everything would be all right. But the big ones never wanted their mothers with them. They were all much too independent these days. They grew up far too quickly. Tom had seen those sweet, little children, with cheeky cherubim faces turn into adults almost overnight. But they weren't adults. They were still children.

They didn't want the swings and slides anymore, either. Not many big ones walked through the park. Most were probably off to buy cigarettes and hang around street corners. Tom shook his head. He shouldn't be so cynical. They weren't all like that. He thought about Sam, smiling as she came closer and closer. Sam wasn't like that.

"Hello, Mr Park Keeper," she said, with that lovely, innocent smile.

Tom couldn't help but laugh. He had asked her to call him Tom, but she seemed to like Mr Park Keeper best. Then his laughter stopped, as it always did, as she waved her goodbye and headed for the swings. She would sit there and swing to and fro as if she hadn't a care in the world, as if she had no idea of what was to come. But she did. And it was getting worse.

The name-calling had been bad enough, but that was just boys.

"Stinky Sam, Smelly Sam," went the chant.

But Sam just sat there on the swings, up and down, up and down she would go.

Then came the spitting, followed by the throwing of sticks. Tom had put a stop to both, but they only seemed to find something worse.

"There she is," the voices shouted.

Daniel and Jack. They were here. Tom edged closer to the swings. The boys were faster. They went right up to the swings and this time, they pushed Sam to the ground. She fell flat on her face, screaming out as gravel grazed her skin. By the time Tom got to her, Daniel and Jack were off, laughing loudly, pushing and shoving one another.

"Sam, oh Sam. Here's a tissue," Tom said, helping her up.

Tom looked at her face, all swollen and sore, at her hands and knees, bleeding and bruised.

"I'd like to get those two banned from the park. But Daniel's dad is on the council. I've not a chance. It might be a good idea if you don't come to the park anymore," Tom said.

He looked down at that face as it battled not to cry.

"They'd find somewhere else to get me," Sam said, gulping back a tear.

"Are they like this to you at school?" Tom said.

"No. They're in different classes. They're not so bad on their own," she said, sounding stronger, "I'm not going to stop coming to the park. I shan't let them stop me doing something I want to do. I shan't. And deep down, they don't really mean it. Deep down, they're like you and me."

Tom closed his eyes. How could she say that? How could she be so forgiving? Tom felt something soft touch his hand. He opened his eyes and looked down. Her hand was in his.

"Thank you, Mr Park Keeper. But I'm all right," Sam said.

She stooped, wincing at the pain, picked up her school bag and was on her way. Tom stood, rooted to the spot for a long time, even after she had faded from view. Then he shook his head.

"What to do? What to do?" he said.

But Tom didn't have to worry about what to do for a while. Sam still came to the park every day, but Daniel and Jack didn't come anymore. Tom was so relieved. Perhaps they had found another route home or perhaps they had changed their ways. Tom knew otherwise. More likely they had found another poor person to terrorize.

Then one day, they came. And Tom saw why they hadn't been for a while. Sam was sat on her swing, as usual. Jack came first. Ever so slowly. His face was a picture of pain and concentration as he gripped the stick at his side and shuffled his feet.

"Jack was in a car accident," Sam said, "he's only just come back to school. He's doing very well, isn't he?"

Tom was about to reply when chants and taunts filled the air.

"Come on, hop-a-long, hurry up. Oh, sorry. You can't, can you?" Daniel laughed.

He was at Jack's side, prodding and poking at him.

"Only old men need walking sticks," another boy said, joining Daniel.

Daniel pushed Jack harder this time. Jack fought for his balance. Just as he regained it, Daniel snatched the stick away. Jack fell to the ground, clutching his leg. Daniel threw the stick at Jack, then turned and sprinted off in the other direction with his friend in tow.

Tom had tried so hard to get there in time. So had Sam. She was at Jack's side first.

"It's all right," she said, stroking Jack's arms. "Is your leg going to be okay? Do you want us to fetch the doctor?"

Jack stared at Sam, the pain of his leg forgotten for a moment as pain of a different kind filled his face.

"You shouldn't care about me. You should be laughing like Daniel and his new mate. We were horrible to you. I was horrible to you. You should hate me."

"I don't hate anyone," Sam said, "I know you didn't mean it really."

"I don't know why I did it. I can't blame Daniel. Yes, it was his idea, but I didn't have to do it. I could have stuck up for you. I could have stopped him," Jack said, "but I can see now. I can see how awful it was. I was a bully. A horrid, horrid bully."

Then he started to cry. His shoulders shook and his head slumped forward.

"Don't cry. Please don't cry. I'll help you home. And I could wait for you after school. Then we could walk through the park together. Two against two. We'll show that Daniel," Sam said.

"You'd do that for me?" Jack said.

He turned his blotchy face towards her.

Sam nodded. "Of course," she said, taking his hand.

"No one's ever done anything like that for me," Jack said.

Tom sniffed and both faces turned towards him. He yanked a handkerchief from his pocket.

"Must be the pollen," he said, dabbing at his eyes.

He helped Jack to his feet and watched as the unlikely pair headed for home. Daniel and his friend would be back. Who knew what would happen then? Though, he had heard a rumour that Daniel's dad had been replaced. Apparently he was a bit of a bully. Perhaps it was time to put that ban into action.

Tom sighed. Yes, he'd do that, but another Daniel would come along. There were too many of them in the world. Then Tom smiled. Indeed, there were, but thankfully, there were also some Sams.

Letters to Santa

July 20th

Dear Santa,

I know it's really early to be writing to you about what I want for Christmas, but something totally horrid has happened. Daddy says that this year, my Christmas present is going to be a baby brother. I want a 3DS and some Moshi Monster stuff. I hate babies. And I hate boys. They're smelly and loud. So, please, please can I have a 3DS and some Moshi Monster stuff and not a baby brother? Thank you.

Love Lauren Prout, aged 6 ¼

September 16th

Dear Santa,

I wrote to you in July about what I wanted and what I didn't want for Christmas. I want a 3DS and some Moshi Monster stuff and I don't want a baby brother. But I don't think you got my letter because my mummy's tummy is really, really fat now and Daddy says my baby brother is in there. Please, please don't give me a baby brother for Christmas. Mummy's belly button is poking outwards and everything. It's yuck.

Love Lauren Prout, aged 6 ½

October 30th

Dear Santa,
Please, please ignore my last letters. I do want my baby brother. I don't care about a 3DS or Moshi Monster stuff. Josh came very early and he's not very well. Mummy and Daddy keep crying. I don't think Josh is going to be OK. Please make him OK.

Love Lauren Prout, aged 6 ½

December 26th

Dear Santa,
Thank you very much for making my baby brother better for Christmas. Josh is very smelly and very loud but I love him. And you gave me a 3DS and Moshi Monster stuff, too. Daddy says I've got to be good for a whole year now. I'll try.

Love Lauren Prout, aged 6 ¾

A New Beginning

The young woman shrank back in her seat, her jagged nails chewing into the cheap cloth. The train charged onwards, oblivious.

"No," she cried, her blue eyes dancing like wondrous waves higher and higher as the man came closer.

Eyes turned to her. Watching. Waiting.

"Tickets, please," the man said.

The woman dared to breathe once more, releasing a girlish giggle from within.

"Everything all right, miss?" the ticket collector said.

"Yes. I thought you were someone else. I'm sorry."

He smiled, punching a hole in her ticket before moving on.

She closed her eyes and Jon's image slowly seeped into her mind. His green eyes snaked round the sockets, searching for her. She gulped. He would have missed her by now. She could see his burly frame, fists flying out at the wall, the door, at anything that stood in his way. She wouldn't rest until she was far, far away.

She wondered why she hadn't left before. Love? Fear?

A tear trickled down her cheek. It had been that last

punch that had decided her. She had told him she was doing overtime at the shop and that she would be home late. He hadn't believed her. He never did. She had coped with the slaps and verbal abuse. Not the stomach though. Not the punch that robbed her of the life growing inside.

Her eyelids drooped, rocking in time with the lull of the train. Sleep beckoned and with it, came dreams of a new beginning.

About the Author

Esther Newton's love affair with writing came about as a result of an accident, where she could no longer carry out her job working in a bank. That accident was the best thing that's happened to her!

She has now been working as a freelance writer for fifteen years, regularly writing articles and short stories for magazines and newspapers such as *Freelance Market News, Writers' Forum, The New Writer, The Guardian, Best of British, The Cat, Woman's Weekly, The People's Friend* and *My Weekly* to name a few.

Winner of *Writing Magazine, Writers' News* and several other prestigious writing competitions and awards, She has also had the privilege of judging writing competitions.

Esther has just finished a series of children's books, which she is now in the process of editing.

As well as working as a freelance writer, Esther has branched out into the exciting world of copywriting, providing copy for sales letters, brochures, leaflets, slogans and e-mails.

She loves writing but equally, Esther enjoys helping

others, which she achieves in her role as tutor for The Writers Bureau. She has also started a blog, designed to provide writers with support, market information and advice: esthernewtonblog.wordpress.com

Lightning Source UK Ltd.
Milton Keynes UK
UKOW05f0425281014

240675UK00002BA/37/P